About the Author

JOHN TAIT was born in Greenock, Scotland, and received his early education there. At the age of seventeen he came to Canada. In the following year, 1914, he enlisted in the 16th Battalion of the Canadian Scottish Regiment and saw four years of war service in England, Belgium and France. He was wounded, and in 1919 received a medical discharge. In 1921 he married Ruperta Bent of Tupperville, N.S., living in Halifax for two years and in New York for the next ten. They returned to Tupperville in 1933, where he lived until his death in 1955. It was in Tupperville, during one of his periodic confinements to bed, that he began to write, and eventually his work started to appear in *Collier's*, *American* and other U.S. magazines; in *National Home Monthly*, *Weekend*, and on the CBC; and in *The Family Herald and Weekly Star* in the stories that constituted his steadiest success. His "Grandma" stories were extensively reprinted abroad in British, Australian, Dutch, Belgian and other magazines.

GRANDMA
takes a hand

GRANDMA
takes a hand

JOHN TAIT

Illustrations by
Adrian Dingle, A.R.C.A.

THE RYERSON PRESS ~ TORONTO

Published 1956

ACKNOWLEDGMENT

I should like to express my deepest gratitude and indebtedness to all who have made the publication of my husband's book possible; especially to Ernest Buckler for his unflagging support whenever advice or assistance was needed.

—RUPERTA TAIT

PRINTED AND BOUND IN CANADA
BY THE RYERSON PRESS, TORONTO

Contents

List of Illustrations

GRANDMA
. . . and the Great Science

IN THE Scotland of my youth it was expected of a boy that, by twelve, he would have formed some idea of what he wanted to do to earn his bread, but in my case ambition at that age had taken me no farther than the crow's nest of a whaler or the saddle of a cow pony.

It was this lamentable state of affairs that brought about a minor crisis within my family circle.

Disgraceful, my mother said that day at dinner, her face troubled; my marks at school were terrible and I didn't seem to care for anything but games and these trashy penny books.

Worse than disgraceful, my father said, squinting at me with menace; if I didn't look slippy and make up my mind what I wanted to do I'd end my days working in somebody's office for twenty-five shillings a week—a fate, I gathered, worse than death.

And it was then that Grandma, who was visiting us at the time, thrust herself into the situation. They didn't need to fash themselves about me, she declared; there was no question whatever about my future. As any phrenologist would tell them, my high forehead and well-rounded cranium, indications of great intellectual and moral force, pointed in one direction only—to the ministry.

Sensation!

1

But at the same time, I saw and understood the consternation on my parents' faces. Suddenly, they were in a ticklish position . . .

Actually, the reading of character by the conformation of the skull had long been out of fashion in Scotland by the time I was born, but neither the light of greater knowledge nor the chill of public ridicule had weakened my maternal grandmother's faith in what she referred to as the "Great Science of Phrenology." At the age of seventeen she had been taken to have her "bumps" read with, I can only suppose, such felicitous results that she had remained forever a passionate, even dogmatic, advocate of the "Science."

But even as a very small boy I had never been much impressed by Grandma's sweeping claims for the "Great Science." In the interests of peace, my parents were careful never to let her know how they felt about her beliefs, but it was obvious to me that they were far from sharing them, and I, naturally, took my attitude from them.

But for all that, I respected Grandma and, contrary to what might have been expected, loved her. She was a tall, gaunt woman with cold slate-grey eyes sunk in deep bony sockets, and a grim mouth. Invariably she dressed in unrelieved black, perpetual mourning for my grandfather, and with her crisp, almost testy, manner must have been rather a forbidding personality.

Yet I never had any fear of her. Autocratic, humourless and completely undemonstrative though she was, I was somehow aware of her warm regard for me and always welcomed her on her periodic visits to our home in Angusburg. . . .

"Aye, a minister," she said now in a voice that dared contradiction. "That's what the Lord intended him for."

I have an idea that eventually my mother could have been won over to support of this notion; the Scots of her time and class had a deep respect for the ministry. But my father rejected it. With tact, however. Grandma was no doubt quite right, he said, but he was afraid she had overlooked certain less admirable elements in my character which tended to invalidate such a conclusion. He went on to particularize.

Grandma cut the invidious recital short. He must be daft, she charged, to expect a big, healthy laddie to be anything but wild and "camsteary." Take her Edward (my uncle Ted):

2

a perfect wee fiend he had been all through his school days, never out of mischief and never opening a book except when driven to it. But now look at him—a steady, hard-working physician. (She didn't mention whether by benefit of phrenology.)

My father, a hardy soul, had the temerity to suggest that perhaps this was the exception rather than the rule, and would have raised further objections, but Grandma silenced him peremptorily. There was no need for argument, Robert. Since he chose to doubt her judgment there was just one thing to be done—take me to a phrenologist and get *his* opinion.

My father exchanged glances with my mother, and I saw pink creep into his face. Now he was in a really awkward spot. It was out of the question to tell Grandma at this late date that he disbelieved utterly in the "Great Science," yet should he agree to a reading he would be more or less committed to an acceptance of its findings. Oh, well, he temporized, we'd see, we'd see. There was no hurry.

Grandma contradicted him flatly. My bumps were as well developed now as they would ever be, she said, and the sooner I saw a phrenologist the better.

But where would they find a phrenologist? my father said reasonably. Unless in one of the large cities—which would mean taking me out of school and an expensive trip, besides. The only phrenologists he had ever seen around Angusburg were the dubious characters who came at fair time and gave readings in a tent at sixpence a head. Could it be one of *them* she was thinking of?

Grandma said with asperity that he knew perfectly well she was thinking nothing of the kind, and thereupon let the subject drop. But none of us believed for an instant that we had heard the last of it. Sooner or later, we knew, Grandma would have my bumps in the hands of an expert. And we could only hope that it would be later—much, much later.

But as fate decreed, it was to be sooner. It was less than a week after that that Grandma returned from a trip into town just in time to join us at tea. She took the cup mother handed her, sugared it, stirred it carefully, and then looked up at my father with a little gleam in her deep-set eyes.

"Weel, Robert, ma braw mannie," she said. "I hae news

3

for ye." This lapse into the vernacular, her own concept of waggishness, was indicative of self-satisfaction.

"News?" my father said, a little uneasily.

"Aye, Robert—news. You'll be happy to know that I've found a phrenologist."

My parents' eyes met and clung.

"A phrenologist, Mamma?" my mother said.

"Just that, Jessie—a phrenologist. Right in the town of Angusburg. Right under our very noses, you might say."

"In Angusburg! But, Mamma, surely you must be mistaken?"

"No, not mistaken," Grandma said flatly. "Although he's presently in the coal business."

My mother looked at my father.

"Who is he?" my father said.

"Name of MacGillivray. Professor Herbert MacGillivray. Well up in his profession at one time, they tell me."

"MacGillivray?" my father said. "In Angusburg?"

"In Angusburg. 2 Harbour Terrace."

"Oh." My father nodded slowly. "That'll be that new coal agency. What's this MacGillivray—the manager?"

" 'Professor' MacGillivray, Robert," Grandma said sternly. "I don't know what he is."

"Then you haven't met him yet?"

"Not yet. But I'm writing tonight for an appointment. For some *Saturday*," Grandma added with an emphasis that warned my father not to raise any trivial objections.

"But, Mamma," my mother said, "he may not be practicing now."

"Maybe not, Jessie." Grandma's grim mouth tightened. "But practicing or no', I mean to see him."

My mother looked appealingly at my father. He shook his head slightly and gave a little helpless shrug. There was just nothing to be done. . . .

If, during the next forty-eight hours, my parents were buoyed up by the hope that the "Professor" would ignore Grandma's letter or refuse to see her, they were to be disappointed. The "Professor" not only replied, but also expressed himself as being delighted with the prospect of serving her and, if it were convenient to her, would hold himself at her disposal on the afternoon of Saturday the twelfth inst.

4

Up to this point I had found the whole situation more amusing than anything else, but now that the interview with the phrenologist had become an actuality, I began to share my parents' alarm. Like them, I knew nothing whatever about the mechanics of the "Great Science," and, again like them, I took it for granted that the "Professor's" conclusions would tally exactly with Grandma's. And that would be bad. Grandma's personal opinions we might conceivably disregard, but Grandma backed by the authority of the "Great Science," an authority none of us had ever denied, would be irresistible— and no vocation appealed less to me right then than that of a minister.

My father was always home on Saturday afternoons. As Grandma and I started down the pathway on our way to town, I glanced back and saw him and my mother watching us gloomily from the sitting room window. And so great was Grandma's force of character that it never even occurred to me to wonder why they didn't just defy her.

No. 2 Harbour Terrace turned out to be a squat two-storey house of what had once been white sandstone, set flush with the pavement. Worn stone steps flanked by rust-eaten iron railings led up to a battered double door, one of whose halves stood ajar. In the window to the left of the door a cardboard sign bearing the legend, "Marine Coalers, Ltd., Office," hung askew from the middle sash. In the window to the right, lace curtains framed a dejected-looking fern in a glistening majolica pot.

I saw Grandma's mouth draw down at the corners as she looked at this unimposing façade, but without hesitation she marched up the steps and pushed the half-door open with the point of her umbrella. We crossed a small vestibule, passed through another doorway, and found ourselves in a bare hallway with walls painted a revolting shade of green. Doors with cracked and faded hand-graining faced each other from either side of us, and to the rear a narrow uncovered stairway hugged one wall. This, I gathered from Grandma's expression, was a far cry from the phrenological parlours of her youth.

At the far end of the staircase there was another door. As we stood looking around, it opened and a face topped by a loose bun of straggling black hair appeared around the jamb and stared at us with squinted black eyes.

5

"I'm looking for Professor MacGillivray," Grandma said abruptly.

"Professor Mac—oh!" Grinning, the woman emerged and came toward us. "It's no' aboot yer bumps, is it?" she said, as though she found the idea mildly entertaining.

"Is Professor MacGillivray in?" Grandma said coldly.

"Aye, he's in, right enough," the woman said with undampened affability. "But he's gone oot o' the bump business. Now, if it was coals ye were wantin'—"

"I have an appointment with him," Grandma said sharply. "For this afternoon."

"Ye have?" The woman clicked her tongue. "Weel, the auld fuiter! He musta forgotten."

I didn't hear Grandma's reply. A chink of light from a crack in the panel of the door to my left had caught my attention and I was peering through it. I saw a stout elderly man in shirtsleeves sitting at a paper-littered table. A short clay pipe barely cleared the fringes of his ragged grey mustache, and he was hurriedly engaged in stowing a flat bottle in the drawer before him.

As he closed the drawer he turned and stared fixedly in my direction, and for a startled instant I thought he had seen me; then it came to me that he was merely listening to the voices behind me.

A sharp tap on my shoulder from Grandma brought me around, and I saw that the woman was opening the door on the opposite side of the hall.

"Weel, away in an' sit ye doon," she said cheerily. "I'll have him here in two shakes o' a lamb's tail, see if I don't."

Grandma led the way past her in unbending silence, and the door closed behind us. The room we were in had the stale fusty odour of disuse, and I heard Grandma sniff fastidiously. But even so it was a marked improvement on what we had seen of the rest of the house.

Its furnishing consisted of a good, though rather worn, Turkey carpet, a sofa and several assorted chairs, and a small elaborately carved desk of some dark wood. Above the sofa there was a large steel etching of the "Charge of the Light Brigade," and opposite it, above a small tiled fireplace, a chart showing a crudely drawn human head in profile, its expression

6

coldly cynical, its hairless cranium neatly divided into sections and labeled, as on a butcher's chart.

Grandma was perched stiffly on the edge of the sofa and I was studying the faintly macabre chart, when the door opened and a man came in. He was wearing a black frock coat that strained across his bulging abdomen and a "stand-up" collar with a black silk cravat. He had thin grey hair brushed straight back from his forehead and a heavy mustache waxed to needle points. It was a moment or two before I recognized him.

"Good-afternoon, Madam." He bowed and then came toward us. "Mrs. Guthrie, I presume?"

Grandma inclined her head a quarter of an inch. "How do you do?" she said austerely. "I understand you forgot our appointment?"

The "Professor" seemed a little taken aback, but recovered at once. "Oh, not at all, Mrs. Guthrie." Plump hands thrust the thought away. "My housekeeper was jumping to conclusions. I saw no need to inform her of your coming." He beamed down at me. "This, of course, will be the laddie you mentioned in your letter," he said, and his breath spoke eloquently of the bottle I had seen him hiding.

"Yes." Grandma's tone had moderated, and I guessed that she was rather impressed by the "Professor's" appearance and manner. "My grandson."

"Indeed? A fine upstanding lad, Mrs. Guthrie. About fifteen, I suppose?"

"Twelve past." Grandma looked at me with severity, concealing her pleasure. "He's well enough—when he behaves himself."

"Ah, yes." He laughed gently. "He's young. A good fault and one that time will correct." He rubbed his hands briskly. "Well, now. Just what was it you had in mind, Mrs. Guthrie? There's the medium examination and the full examination. And then if you wished a chart filled out—"

Grandma's hand cut him short. "What I want you to do is examine this boy and tell me what he's best fitted for in life."

"Ah-hah." The "Professor" stroked his cheek. "That would require the full examination, of course. I take it, then, that he has shown no special leaning as yet?"

7

"Only the usual daft-like notions." Grandma gave a little snort. "A detective!" she said, referring to my latest aspiration.

"The boy of it, the boy of it. And yet, Mrs. Guthrie, we may find that a detective is exactly what he ought to be."

"Nonsense!" Grandma said. "I know enough about phrenology to tell me that, Professor MacGillivray."

"Indeed?" The "Professor's" tone implied surprise and interest. "Then surely you must have arrived at some opinion regarding his future?"

"I have that," Grandma said. "I'm firmly of the opinion that he should study—" Her lips clamped together. "But there. It might be as well first to hear *your* opinion."

"Just as you say, Madam." It seemed to me that the "Professor's" voice had chilled. He drew one of the chairs over by the window. "If you'll just sit here, sonny."

I sat down facing the window and waited with mingled amusement and apprehension for the reading to begin. Through the begrimed foliage of a sycamore outside the house I could catch glimpses of a busy dock and, beyond it, of yachts lying at their moorings in the bay.

The "Professor" went over to the desk and came back with a tape measure. He began to measure my head, all the way around, over the top from base of nose to occipital bone, over the top from ear to ear, around the front from ear to ear, around the back from ear to ear. As he measured he mumbled the figures to himself and little puffs of alcoholic fragrance drifted down to my nostrils.

The measuring over, the "Professor" placed his finger tips at the middle of my forehead and began to move them towards my temples with a slow rotating movement. They paused as they encountered the bony swellings above my eyes.

"Ah." I could feel him turn to Grandma. "Perceptiveness —very highly developed. He'll not miss much, this laddie."

"No." Grandma's voice was grim. "Not if he's supposed to miss it."

The reading went on with a running commentary from the "Professor." It seemed that I was possessed of an astonishing number of desirable qualities, and behind me I could hear Grandma's little grunts of approval and satisfaction. "And now." The "Professor" came around and looked down at me thoughtfully. "We come to a choice of vocation. Tell me,

8

"Ah!" I could feel him turn to Grandma.
"Perceptiveness—very highly developed."

sonny—while I was examining you, you were listening to what I said, weren't you?"

"Yes, sir," I said.

"But at the same time you were looking out the window. What were you looking at?"

I told him I had been looking at the top of a dockside crane that rose above and beyond the sycamore tree.

"Can you describe it to me without looking at it again?"

I said I thought I could, and did so.

"There!" He turned to Grandma. "You can see the significance of that, Mrs. Guthrie? He not only possesses great perceptiveness, but he also has a photographic sense of form. He sees without knowing that he sees, and yet is able to recall what he has seen."

Grandma made no reply, and I glanced around at her. She was staring up at the "Professor", her eyes hard and bright. "You're not going to tell me he ought to be a detective?" she said ominously.

"Oh, dear me, no!" The "Professor" smiled. "That would be a sad misapplication of ability. No, there remains no doubt about the field of endeavour in which his future should lie."

"Yes?" Grandma sounded dubious.

"Without question, Madam, somewhere in the field of creative art."

"Art!" Grandma spat the word. "Is that what you'd make of him—a feckless paint dauber?"

The "Professor's" eyelids fluttered at the wrath in her voice. "Well, not—not necessarily, Madam." He turned and looked out the window as though seeking inspiration. And, I have always believed, found it. "Something more utilitarian, I think," he said, turning back to her. "Yacht designing, for instance, would be very near it."

"I . . . see." There was something awful in Grandma's voice and in the way she rose from the sofa. She took her purse from her handbag and opened it. "Your fee, sir?"

The "Professor" looked at her for an instant with protest on his large face. Then it turned wooden. "Five shillings, if you please, Madam," he said tonelessly.

Grandma took two half-crowns from her purse and handed them to him. "Come!" she said to me, and without another word marched from the room. . . .

10

For all her crusty exterior, I had never known Grandma to be harsh or unkind to me, yet as I trotted beside her on the way home I had a feeling that it would be wiser to venture neither remark nor comment. In unbroken silence we reached the house, and I waited docilely while she removed her outdoor things and then followed her into the sitting room. My parents were there, strain in their faces, obviously waiting to hear the worst.

Without so much as a glance at them, Grandma marched over to the table, picked up her knitting, and sat down, stiffly erect, on the edge of a straight chair, her face a dour uninformative mask.

My father looked at her for a moment, questioningly, and then turned to me with lifted eyebrows.

I glanced hesitantly at Grandma. "I'm to be a yacht designer," I said subduedly.

My father's eyes widened, and then I saw his mouth twitch.

"A—a yacht designer?" he said unsteadily, and looked at my mother, who was suddenly biting furiously at her lower lip. "Well, well! That's a worthy occupation, Dunc."

Grandma's flying needles stopped abruptly. "Havers!" she rasped. "The man's nothing but an old blether."

"Oh, surely not?" my father said seriously. "He's an expert, you know. Well up in his profession at one time."

Grandma glowered at him. "He's an expert gowk, Robert. But since you prefer to take his word instead of mine—well, we'll just wait and see who's right."

"Good idea," my father said agreeably. "After all, time will tell."

GRANDMA

. . . and the Sassenach

I WAS so full of the half-panicky, half-exhilarating excitement of flight as I raced up the pathway to Grandma's cottage that I failed to see the stocky figure of Mr. MacCauley, the postman, coming from the door. We collided and the sheaf of letters he was holding went flying.

"Gracious, laddie!" he said vexedly but with commendable self-restraint, as we unscrambled ourselves. "A body would think the de'il was after ye."

Stammering an apology I helped him to retrieve his letters and then went on into the house. Grandma was in the sitting room, her long gaunt frame perched stiffly on the edge of a straight chair, an unopened letter in her hand. She watched me cross the room and sit down, her face dour and unsmiling as always, and I knew she had witnessed my precipitate entrance.

"Humph!" she said, with a wealth of hidden eloquence.

I brushed my hand across my moist forehead. "It's real warm out today, Grandma."

"Aye." Her voice was dry, and she glanced with cold deeply-set grey eyes at the deserted roadway and beach. " 'The guilty flee when no man pursueth.' What have you on your conscience?"

"Nothin'," I said.

12

She said "Humph!" again and searched my face with keen old eyes. "There's a bruise on your cheek. Is it fighting you've been up to?"

I knew then that I'd have to tell her. Not that I minded, really. No matter how gruff and undemonstrative she might be, I knew I didn't have a better friend than Grandma, and I was never happier than during the summer months when the holidays made it possible for me to stay with her.

"It wasn't my fault," I said. "He hit me first."

"Who did?"

"This chap. He stopped me down the road there. 'Where are you going, you dirty ragamuffin?' he says."

Grandma's eyes dropped to the worn and mended jacket, breeks and shoes which, in the sacred name of economy, she always insisted I "get the wear of" while visiting her. Ardrach, she would point out, wasn't one of your high-toned summer resorts, and so long as I was clean, a few patches didn't matter.

"It was ill said," she observed. " 'Whoso mocketh the poor reproacheth his Maker.' So what happened?"

"I told him to go to the blazes and he said I better keep a civil tongue in my head. Then the man said, 'That's it, son. Don't take any lip off the beggar'."

"Bless us! What man?"

"The man sitting in the front garden. So this Bert said, 'You better clear out of here before you get one on the eye.' 'Who's going to give it to me?' I said. 'You?' And the man said, 'Go on, Bert. Pop him one on his cheeky Scotch nose'."

"Scotch nose?" Flame kindled in Grandma's eyes. "What man was this?"

"Some Englishman. In that white stone house by the bridge."

"Major Ponsonby!" Grandma's voice was harsh with dislike. "A big stout body with a face like a Dunlop cheese?"

"Only redder," I said. "And a big white mustache."

She breathed deeply through distended nostrils. "Well, upon my soul! The cheek of the thing! What happened then?"

"Well, this Bert came at me and bashed me one on the cheek. Then I landed one on him and he stopped and began to greet like a bairn. Then the man called me a bad name and came out to me, and I had to run for it."

Grandma had turned her head away. "Tuts, laddie!" she

13

said, "you shouldna have struck back. You might have hurt the poor creature." But I could hear the gratification in her voice.

"I did hurt him," I boasted, ignoring the fact that a combination of fear and luck, rather than cold skill, had guided my fist. "I bashed him one on the nose and made it bleed."

"Shame on you," Grandma said, but without conviction. "It's an ill thing to take pleasure in hurting a fellow creature. Even a poor thrawn thing of a Sassenach."

"It was his own fault," I defended myself.

Grandma turned. "It was his father's fault—the impertinent Sassenach blackguard. Only a renter here for the summer and behaving as if he'd bought the place!"

"Then they don't belong here?" I said.

"Belong here!" Grandma snorted. "No Englishman belongs anywhere in Scotland—though you'd never ken it to see them, with their strutting and their lah-di-dah airs. But that's the Sassenach for you: I tell you, laddie, for six hundred years they've been the curse of Scotland, and it's a wonder to me the Lord hasn't smitten them as He smote the oppressors of Israel. . . ."

There was a lot more in the same vein, all of it an old story to me. Grandma, a Jacobite at heart, was firmly of the opinion that the English were a human sub-species who, having discovered that force could avail them nothing against the superior fighting qualities of the Scots, had, by the exercise of treachery and low cunning, succeeded in making themselves masters of the land. I waited patiently for her to run down.

"Who's your letter from, Grandma?" I said, breaking in at the first opportunity.

She glanced down at it as if she had forgotten it. "Lawyer Gilmour," she said with distaste. "Sleekit wee rascal—what does he want of me?"

I watched with no great interest while she opened the letter and read it.

"My faith!" She looked up at me, her eyes hard and bright. "He tells me he thinks he can sell 'Craigfell' and wants me to name a figure."

"Craigfell," a two-storey house of red sandstone located on the other side of Ardrach, was the home where Grandma had raised her family, including my mother. But the children

14

had found homes of their own, my grandfather had died, and Grandma, alone now, had closed it up and bought the small cottage in which she now lived. Since then "Craigfell" had stood empty, awaiting a buyer.

"Who's going to buy it?" I said.

She grunted. "Catch Gilmour lettin' on about that before he has to! He's not so daft." She squinted her eyes, peering at me but not seeing me. "It's not worth a penny more than five hundred pounds," she mused, "but I'd best be on the safe side and say six."

"Why?" I said, from the depths of my business ignorance. "If it's only worth five hundred why not say five hundred?"

Her eyes came back to me, round and bright in their deep sockets. "Laddie," she said, "if you're ever in business there's one thing you'll do well to learn—you can lower your price but never raise it." She squinted again. "Forbye, there's just the chance that I might get six hundred." . . .

So far as I was concerned, my encounter with Major Ponsonby and his son was a thing finished and done with and, like the little animal I was, I dismissed it from my mind. But as was soon to become evident, fate had other ideas.

The next afternoon I was on my way back from a trip along the beach, laden with a large dead crab, a cork float, half a dozen shark eggs and various other treasures, when, just as I drew near Grandma's cottage, I became aware of heavy footsteps coming up rapidly behind me. As they drew near me I glanced around idly. And then I stopped short, frozen.

"Hah!" A large beefy hand closed on the collar of my jacket and spun me around, and I found myself staring affrightedly into the angry and crimson face of Major Ponsonby. "Confounded little guttersnipe!" he grated. "I've been hoping to get my hands on you."

My gleanings of the afternoon fell and scattered around my feet as, terrified, I began to struggle. "Let me alone!" I yelled. "Let go of me!"

The Major paid no attention but began to shake me. "Strike my boy, will you, you dirty little Scotch blighter! By Gad, I'll teach you to respect your betters, I will."

He was shaking me so violently now that further speech was impossible, my vision reduced to a crazy whirling. Then amidst the whirling I caught a fragmentary glimpse of Grandma

15

Behind him, grey eyes ablaze, the umbrella poised in readiness, stood an ancient fury whom I recognized as Grandma.

staring from her doorway and, an instant or two later, another glimpse of her advancing across the lawn, an umbrella in her hand, her face black with rage.

The first intimation either the Major or I had of her immediate presence was a dull, heavy whack. I was released then, and I staggered back and saw him standing motionless, his arms half raised, his bowler crushed in and driven down over his eyes. Behind him, grey eyes ablaze, the umbrella poised in readiness, stood an ancient fury whom I scarcely recognized as Grandma.

The Major came suddenly to life. Wrenching at the battered bowler he spun around. Then I saw something between rage and amazement fill his face. "Why, you—you old harridan! How dare you! Are you out of your mind?" he blared.

The umbrella quivered threateningly. "Away! Away, you abominable Sassenach bully, and leave my grandson be!"

"Your grandson!" Obviously, the Major was taken aback. No matter what extremes of conduct circumstances might lead her to, Grandma was unmistakably a lady, and it hadn't occurred to him that we might be related.

"Aye, my grandson," snapped Grandma. "Patches and all. But no matter who he is, what right have you, a grown man, to abuse him? Or is it the way in England for men to go around cloutin' wee boys?"

"You're talking rot, ma'am." The Major was almost shouting. "Do you realize that this—this young rascal struck my son and nearly broke his nose? By Gad, what he deserves —" He broke off with an odd bleating sound as the point of the umbrella buried itself in his bulging middle.

"Blasphemer!" Grandma's voice was outraged. "You'd dare to stand there and take the Lord's name in vain!"

The Major's face convulsed. He snatched the umbrella from Grandma's hand and smashed it down across the top of the gate-post. "Confounded old virago!" he snarled and threw the wreck at her feet. "If you were a man I'd knock you down."

Shock in her face, Grandma stared down at the umbrella as he strode away, and then stooped slowly and picked it up. It was ruined, a rib poking through the torn silk in a compound fracture.

17

"My best umbrella," she said with grief. "The last thing your grandfather gave me." Rage blazed suddenly in her face. "Och, the Sassenach messin! What I should have taken to him was the poker."

"Will he not have to pay for it?" I said.

"Aye, will he. And pay dear. It's there in the Book: Ye shall not afflict an widow or fatherless child. If thou afflict them in any wise, and they cry at all unto me, I will surely hear their cry."

But though I was not sceptical, I wasn't so sure. Somehow, I could hardly see the Lord concerning Himself with anything so trifling as a broken umbrella. . . .

It was easy to see during the next forty-eight hours that all was not well with Grandma. Never at the best of times what you could call lively company, she was even more silent and withdrawn than ever and, in spite of her faith in a special dispensation of Providence on her behalf, I knew she was suffering. But not, I suspected, from the destruction of her umbrella so much as from the thought of having been bested by a despised Sassenach.

On the afternoon of the second day I was busily developing my egg-sized biceps by chinning myself on a low-hanging limb of the plane tree in front of the house, when Mr. MacCauley, the postman, came along.

"Here, Samson," he said, grinning at me through his mustache. "Gie yer muscles a change an' tak this in for me like a good lad."

I took the letter he handed me and went into the house. Grandma was in the kitchen, making marmalade. She glanced at the letter and then paused to swing the burnished copper jam kettle to the back of the range.

"From Gilmour," she said with a grimace, as she sat down and opened it. "What do you bet the wee rascal wants me to take four-fifty for the house?" And then, as she began to read, I saw her lips fall apart and her grey eyes turn bright. "Faith, laddie!" she said. "Listen to this."

She mumbled through the letter's salutation and opening paragraph. Then: " 'My client, a Major Horace Ponsonby who, as you may be aware, has been living in Ardrach this summer and who has newly formed business connections in Glasgow and Paisley, feels that your price is on the high side; however,

18

he is anxious to acquire the property immediately so that the house may be put in condition and he and his family settled in before winter, and is, therefore, willing to accept your figure. This being the case, then, I should be grateful if you or your representative would arrange to be at my office at three o'clock in the afternoon of the 21st inst., bringing all relative instruments. Major Ponsonby, also, will be present so that a transfer may be effected with a minimum of delay'."

"You mean," I said gropingly, "that Major Ponsonby wants you to go there so he can buy 'Craigfell' for six hundred pounds?"

"Just that." There was contempt in Grandma's voice. "The feckless English gowk—more siller than sense."

"But you'll not go?" I said.

"Not go?" Grandma's eyes glinted. "Indeed and I'm going. What way would I not go, pray tell me?"

I lowered my eyes. "I didn't think you'd touch his old money," I mumbled.

She was slow in replying, and I glanced up and saw her watching me, her face rigid and stern, her nostrils flaring, in her a sure sign of amusement.

"Ach, away out and play, you daft bairn," she said, and gave me a little push that I knew was really a caress, the only kind of caress she ever permitted herself. "I'll write to Gilmour as soon as I get the marmalade done, and maybe if you're a good laddie I'll let you go with me."

Which was little consolation. For I was disappointed in her. Already I had been inculcated with the doctrine that business is business, regardless of sentiment; but there is no one more idealistic than a small boy and it hurt me to see Grandma grasping eagerly for the money of a man who had abused and insulted her and whom she utterly despised.

And any frail hope I may have cherished that she would change her mind was shattered the next afternoon, when she came back from town with a new umbrella, practically the duplicate of the one the Major had smashed.

"Nine shillin's, mind you," she said, as she placed it carefully in the umbrella stand in the hall. "A bonnie price. But then," she added comfortably, "I can well afford to be choosey."

I said nothing. But I was aware of a distinct and painful sense of loss. She was still Grandma and I loved her as much but I felt I would never again be able to regard her with the whole-hearted esteem and admiration I had in the past. . . .

The afternoon of the 21st came and we set out for Lawyer Gilmour's. I was in an almost painful state of cleanliness, scrubbed, combed and arrayed in my Sunday best, and beside me Grandma strode along in funeral black, erect, dignified and, as always when outside her family circle, very much the Scottish lady. Now that we were on our way to meet the Major again, my unhappy disillusionment gave way for the time to anticipation, and as I walked I wondered with excitement, pleasurably tinctured with apprehension, what his reaction would be when he saw whose house he was buying.

Lawyer Gilmour's office was above a butcher's shop in the narrow, twisting, cobbled thoroughfare that was Ardrach's main business street. As we left the stairhead and entered the outer office, a clerk perched on a high stool turned from his desk and then slipped quickly to the floor.

"Mistress Guthrie?"

Grandma nodded curtly.

"If you'll come ben here, Mistress Guthrie," the clerk said, leading the way to a closed door. "Mr. Gilmour and Major Ponsonby are waitin' on you."

The room into which he ushered us was almost square, with one large window facing the street. One wall was lined with a rack bearing black-japanned metal boxes and before the window stood a furnishing that was part desk, part table. Behind this contrivance sat the small, skinny, squint-eyed person of Lawyer Gilmour. In another chair opposite him reposed the generous amplitudes of Major Ponsonby.

As the clerk announced Grandma both men rose, and Lawyer Gilmour came bustling around on immaculate buttoned boots to greet her. But I was watching the Major and as he looked at Grandma I saw with interest the flood of colour that rushed suddenly into his face.

"Good-day to you, Mrs. Guthrie." Gilmour bobbed his head in what passed for a bow. "I'm happy indeed to see you. How have you been keeping?"

"Well, thank you," Grandma said, without enthusiasm.

"Splendid, splendid! I'm extremely glad to hear it." He

20

turned. "May I have the pleasure of introducing our fellow-townsman-to-be, Major Ponsonby?"

"I have already met Major Ponsonby," Grandma said in her iciest voice. "Once."

I saw Gilmour's sharp eyes go from Grandma's granite face to the Major's suffused one, and there was a little awkward pause. Then the lawyer recovered.

"Well, excellent, excellent! I had no idea you were already acquainted." He busied himself in drawing forward another chair. "But sit you down, Mrs. Guthrie, sit you down, and we'll go on with our business."

As he scampered back to his own chair Grandma lowered herself slowly and sat bolt upright, her handbag on her arm, black-gloved hands clasped on the head of her umbrella. I, being a mere juvenile, just wasn't there and was left to stand beside her.

"Well, now." Rubbing his hands briskly, Gilmour sat down. "We'll get on. I take it, Mrs. Guthrie, that you brought—"

"You'll excuse me." Grandma's cold voice cut him off. "There's a matter I wish to take up with Major Ponsonby." She turned glittering eyes on the Major. "The matter of a wantonly destroyed umbrella."

Again the Major flushed darkly, and he hitched uncomfortably in his chair. "Well, really, ma'am," he muttered, "we're no more than even, there. After all, you did destroy my hat."

"With good reason," snapped Grandma. "You were brutally assaulting my grandson here. But you had no reason whatsoever to destroy my umbrella."

"No reason!" The Major bristled. "Gad, ma'am, you stabbed me—"

"That'll do, sir!" Grandma's grey eyes blazed at him. "I've spoken to you before about your blasphemy. What's more, I have no mind to sit and bandy words with you. You know right from wrong as well as I do."

The Major's mouth opened, closed, and he appeared to swallow something.

Gilmour had been fidgeting impatiently. "I know nothing whatever about this disagreement," he said crisply, "but it seems to me, Major, that if it is merely a simple matter of

21

replacing an umbrella you'd do well to get it cleared out of the way."

The Major turned hot eyes on him, and I expected to see the little lawyer blasted with a barrage of angry words. But no words came and after a moment the Major looked away.

"Very well, ma'am," he said in a stifled voice. "I'll replace your umbrella."

"I've already replaced it," Grandma said curtly. She opened her handbag and took out a receipted store bill. "Nine shillin's, it cost me."

In silence the Major took out his purse, found a half-sovereign and placed it on the lawyer's desk. "If you have a shilling, ma'am," he said bleakly.

Grandma took a shilling from her purse and placed it with the bill on the desk. She picked up the half-sovereign, dropped it in her purse, placed the purse in her handbag, closed the handbag, and rose.

"I wish you a good-day, sir," she said to Gilmour.

"But, Mrs. Guthrie!" Gilmour leapt to his feet, dismay on his face. "Our other business."

"There is no other business," Grandma said coldly. "If you'll trouble yourself to read my last letter you'll find that I did nothing more than agree to meet Major Ponsonby."

"But—but—" Spots of colour appeared in the lawyer's lean cheeks. "Madam, this is nothing but a quibble. You expressed your willingness to sell 'Craigfell.' You even quoted a figure—a figure that has been met."

"I'm not denyin' it," said Grandma. "But if you hadn't been so canny about letting on who your client was, I'd have told you then what I'm tellin' you now—that I'll never willingly see any property of mine pass into the hands of a Sassenach." She paused, challenging their blank, bemazed faces with her minatory stare, and then turned abruptly away. "Come, Duncan!"

With a curious mingling of shame and elation I followed her from the room and down the stairway to the street. There she stopped, a little gleam in her eyes.

" 'The evil bow before the good; and the wicked at the gates of the righteous'," she quoted.

"You gave them laldy, didn't you, Grandma?" I said with admiration.

22

"Humph!" She looked down her nose at me. Her nostrils were flaring. "So you're not scunnered at your greedy auld grannie any more?"

I felt heat burn into my face. "You could have told me," I mumbled.

"Aye, so I could." She gave me a little cuff. "But just see what fun I'd have missed. Laddie, could you do with a dish of ice cream?"

And in case the reader should feel that Grandma's ethics in this affair hadn't been the most admirable, it is only fair to add that in church the next Sunday morning I oversaw her slip a half-sovereign in the plate.

GRANDMA
... and the Godly Hamish

THE LETTER for Grandma came on a Saturday afternoon, when both my father and I were home. It had been forwarded from her home and was addressed in a laborious, sprawling hand to: "Mistress Eliza Guthrie, Ardrach, Ayr."

Grandma peered at it briefly with deeply set slate-grey eyes and then handed it to my mother. "Here, Jessie, I left my specs in my room. See who's it from."

My mother opened it and glanced at the subscription. "Hamish Macgregor," she said, and looked inquiringly at Grandma.

"Hamish Macgregor!" Grandma lowered her knitting. "Well, I never! I haven't laid eye on Hamish for more than forty years and I jaloused he was in his grave long ago. What does he say, Jessie?"

"But who is he?" my mother said.

"A laddie I used to know when I was a wee smout of a lassie in Auchterfenty; the youngest son of my father's foreman." She lowered her eyes with an effect of grisly coyness. "Hamish and I had quite a notion of each other at one time, but then he went sailin' and I never saw him again. What does he say, Jessie?"

My mother lifted the letter. " 'Braeside Dock, Glasgow, N.B.'," she read. " 'Dear Lizzie: Just a wee scrape to let you

24

ken that my ship, the Highland Maid, will be laid up here till the end of the month and that if you are willing I will be dropping down to see you. It was only by chance that I happened to hear that your man had gone to his rest, and grieved for you though I was, it garred me think of the old days in Auchterfenty. My, Lizzie, but you were the bonnie, bonnie one, and I have never forgot the time down by the burn when you put your arms around my neck and kissed—' "

"Here!" Grandma snatched the letter from my mother's hand. "The cheek of you, Jessie Mackinley!" she said indignantly. "Have you no respect for the privacy of others?"

"But, Mamma, you told me to read it."

"I told you to read it, aye, but I expected you to use a little ordinary discretion, too." Grandma stuffed the letter in the pocket of her skirt. "I'll read it myself when I go up."

My father smoothed a grin away with his hand. "The Highland Maid?" he said. "What ship is that?"

"You know as much about it as I do, Robert," said Grandma. "But he was a real promisin' lad and I doubt it'll be nothin' less than a liner."

My father shook his head. "I doubt it. More likely a tramp."

"And what if it is?" demanded Grandma. "To be captain of a tramp steamer is still a position of importance and responsibility." She watched her flying needles for a little. "I wonder," she said musingly, "did he ever marry?"

My mother looked at her with dawning alarm. "Why, Mamma? What difference does that make?"

"I didn't say it made any difference," said Grandma. "And I didn't say it didn't."

My parents looked at each other.

"He's an old man now, you know," my father said meaningly.

"Is he, indeed?" snapped Grandma. "And accordin' to you I'm an old woman, I suppose?" She glanced down at her long gaunt frame, stiffly erect on the edge of a straight chair. "Maybe I'm no longer in the first bloom of my youth," she said with dour complacence, "but I havena run to blubber like some I know." A double-barrelled retort, since both my parents were on the plump side.

My mother was looking definitely worried now. "You

don't mean, surely, Mamma, that you'd consider marrying again?"

"What way not?" demanded Grandma. "It's an ill thing for a woman to live by herself, and a braw couthie lad like Hamish might do me fine for my lonely old age."

My mother gave a little sigh of impatience. The truth was that in spite of, or perhaps because of, certain little peculiarities of character Grandma was much loved by her children and never alone. "But, Mamma," she persisted, "you don't really know him now, and I don't have to tell you that sailors are apt to be on the rowdy side."

"Not Hamish," said Grandma firmly. "There never was a more godly lad came out of Auchterfenty. His father was beadle in the kirk and he raised his twelve children to be upright, God-fearin' Christian men and women. . . . But I was thinkin', Jessie—I'd do better to have him come here instead of Ardrach. Then he could stay a week."

My mother gasped. "But Mamma—" She stopped short and looked appealingly at my father. He gave a little helpless shrug.

"Aye?" Grandma was watching her. "But what?"

My mother turned and braved Grandma's minatory stare. "I meant, Mamma, wouldn't it be better to see what he's like before you ask him to stay?"

"Nothin' of the kind, Jessie! The boy is father to the man, and there's little doubt what he'll be like."

"But, Mamma, you never can tell—"

"Whist, girl!" said Grandma sternly. "Either come out with it and tell me my friends are not welcome here or hold your tongue."

My mother sighed then and gave up. Grandma, as usual, would have her way. . . .

Grandma's invitation to her girlhood sweetheart went off in the next post, and as we waited for a reply, I speculated happily on what he would be like. Angusburg, where we lived, was a seaport town and ships' officers were a common sight on its streets. Big burly men for the most part but smart in their gold braid and buttons, they had always been romantic figures to me and I was thrilled at the prospect of meeting one of them.

The expected letter came on the next Friday. This time Grandma guarded it carefully from our eyes, but she informed us that Captain Macgregor would be with us the next day and, my mother would be interested to know, that he was still unmarried.

It was about four o'clock the next afternoon and I was whipping my top on the pavement in front of the house, when I beheld the strange figure approaching me from the direction of town. It was a man with a close-cropped grey beard and flowing mustache, above which protruded an enormous beak of a nose. A battered bowler perched on his shock of grizzled hair and he wore a coarse seaman's jersey, and heavy woollen trousers thrust into high sea boots. Under one arm he carried a canvas kitbag.

"Tell me wance an' tell me true," he said, looking down at me with eyes that contrived to be bold yet somehow sly. "Whaur does Mr. Robert Mackinley live?"

I pointed to the house, wondering. "In there," I said.

"There!" The eyes squinted through the poplars in the front garden. "Man, he must be weel aff."

I didn't know about that. "He's my father," I said.

"Yer faither?" He turned. "Then you'll be Lizzie's grandson?"

The impossible truth came to me then. "You—you're not Captain Macgregor?"

"Aye, but I am, laddie. Jist that. Captain Macgregor of the good ship Highland Maid."

"Is it a liner?" I said.

"A liner!" There was scorn in his voice. "Nane o' yer liners for me. Ye micht as weel run a hotel as a liner. No, laddie, she's a steam puffer an' one o' the cosiest wee ships ye ever laid eye on."

A steam puffer! I thought disappointedly. Hundreds of times I had seen them crawling about the Clyde, dirty little cargo boats with crews of three or four. "Grandma thought it was a liner," I said.

"Did she, noo. Weel, I'll awa' in an' break the guid news to her."

I followed him along the gravel pathway to the front door. It opened as we climbed the steps, and Grandma stood before us, resplendent in black bombazine, her best jet brooch at her throat.

"What's this, Duncan?" she said sharply, eyeing my companion with cold distaste. "If he's beggin' take him round to the back door."

"Michty me!" said the Captain in a voice of awe. "This is never Lizzie?"

I saw fire blaze in Grandma's eyes and then die again as she realized who he was. "It can't be," she said disbelievingly. "It can't be."

The Captain chuckled. "Aye, but it can, Lizzie."

"You mean to tell me you're Hamish Macgregor?"

"Nane other. Would ye no' have kent me?"

Grandma recovered her grim composure abruptly. "I might," she said tartly, "if you'd stopped at the barber's on your way here."

The Captain laughed easily. "Same auld Lizzie," he said. "Ye were aye a lass o' spirit. But ye've changed, yersel'. It's a fine figure o' a woman ye've become, Lizzie."

"Michty me!" said the Captain in a voice of awe.
"This is never Lizzie?"

28

Behind Grandma in the hall I heard my father give a strangled cough.

So did Grandma. Spots of colour in her cheeks, she stood back from the door. "Well, you're here," she said grudgingly, "so I suppose you might as well come in."

"Thanky." Apparently unconscious of any lack of warmth in his welcome, the Captain stepped into the hall. His kitbag he dropped to the floor and then removed the battered bowler and placed it tenderly on the hall table. "An' wha's this bonnie lass?" he said, grinning at my mother.

"My daughter, Jessie," Grandma said tonelessly. "Captain Macgregor, Jessie."

The Captain touched his forelock. "A credit tae ye, Lizzie," he said. "An' no' unlike ye when ye were younger."

"Maybe. And this is my good son, Robert MacKinley."

"Put it there, Robert," said the Captain with vast geniality, and offered a huge and far from immaculate hand. "Ony connection o' Lizzie's is a friend o' mine."

"Thank you, Captain," my father said gravely, and then winced as his fingers were seized in a crushing grip.

Mary Strachan, the maid, was hovering in the background. My mother turned to her. "Mary, will you show Captain Macgregor to his room? . . . Tea in fifteen minutes, Captain."

"Noo ye're talkin'!" said the Captain with enthusiasm, and swooped on his kitbag. "When it comes tae food, Jessie, I'm yer man."

There was silence in the hall as Mary led the way up the stairway. Then as they disappeared around the landing my mother turned to Grandma. "Good heavens, Mamma! And that's your godly Hamish!"

I saw my father's quick nudge of warning, but the damage was already done.

Grandma stiffened, her eyes sparkling. "That'll do you, Jessie. Just because he's a wee thing on the spirited side is no reason to sneer at him."

"I'm not sneering, Mamma. But you know as well as I do that he's coarse and forward and impertinent—impossible!"

Grandma's mouth tightened obstinately. "No doubt you're made of finer dust, Jessie, but he suits me well enough."

I saw my father's mouth twitch. "And you seem to suit him, too," he said gravely. "A fine, fine lad—I can see now where he'll make you a real lively companion for your old age."

The spots of colour came back to Grandma's face and she looked at him with suspicion. "You seem to have changed your tune since the other day?"

My father shrugged. "Circumstances alter cases. I'm sure I'm very happy for both of you."

Grandma stared at him, her lips working, and I thought she was going to blast him; then without speaking she wheeled away and marched into the sitting room and slammed the door.

"Oh, Robert!" my mother said despairingly. "What are we to do?"

"Nothing, Jess. There's nothing we can do."

"You don't really believe she'll marry him?"

"Don't be daft, lass. She wouldn't look at him twice. But it was a mistake, Jess, to run him down that way."

"Oh, I know," my mother said. "But he's so awful— Robert, we simply can't have him here. On Monday the Urquharts are coming to dinner and Tuesday evening the Ogilvies are coming in for whist. What on earth would they think?"

My father grinned. He was never greatly concerned about what people thought. "It might be entertaining to know," he said. "But, anyway, I'm afraid we've just got to put up with it."

30

"But, Robert," my mother wailed, "surely there's some way of getting around her?"

My father shook his head slowly. "You know your mother, Jess. She's taken her stand and now nothing'll move her." . . .

Speaking strictly for myself, that evening was a most enjoyable one. The Captain, it soon developed, was a "lad of parts." At both tea and dinner he displayed a positive virtuosity as a feeder and even my father, who was no mean trencher-man, watched with awe the vast quantities of food that disappeared behind the heavy fringe of mustache.

But it was in the sitting room, after dinner, that his real talents began to emerge. With a self-assurance that was as complete as it was unwarranted, he undertook to entertain us with dubious accounts of his adventures on the deep and then switched to song, which he illustrated with a wealth of graphic gesture.

"How did that suit ye, Robert?" he said, as he finished a touching piece about a boy who, dying on the field of battle, relives the scenes of his childhood.

"Remarkable," my father said solemnly. "A real achievement."

"Aye," said the Captain, and looked at him sidewise, "but if I had a drap or twa I could lift ye richt oot o' yer seat. But there," he added, as my father shook his head, "I'm jist tellin' ye, no' askin'."

Through it all Grandma had been silent, glowering. Now she spoke suddenly. "Hamish, do you have a suit of clothes?"

The Captain turned, surprise on his face. "What way dae ye ask, Lizzie?"

"Because tomorrow's the Sabbath and you'll need somethin' decent for kirk."

"Kirk!" The Captain seemed slightly taken aback. He sat down and rubbed his beard. "What kirk dae ye attend, Lizzie?"

"What other kirk but the one I've always attended—the United Free."

The Captain shook his head somberly. "That wad never dae for me, Lizzie. I've jined the—the Holy Christians."

"The Holy Christians?" Grandma eyed him narrowly. "I never heard of them."

"It's a new sect," the Captain said. "We dinna haud wi' organs an' choirs an' fancy hymn tunes. A' we hae is a precentor an' the auld psalms an' a bit sermon. Jist wan service on the Sabbath an' the rest o' the day we give up tae prayer and soul-searchin'. I'm real put out ye havena Holy Christian kirk in Angusburg."

"I'm sure," said Grandma dryly. "Well, I'm warnin' you, Hamish, if you don't go to kirk you'll spend most of tomorrow alone."

"In prayer and soul-searching," my father added.

The Captain looked quickly at his guileless face. "Aye, jist that, Robert," he said after a moment. "Jist that."

Late that night an earache wakened me, and my mother had to get up and put laudanum drops in my ear. In the morning it was still paining slightly so, as even the maid would be at kirk, it was decided that I should stay home and keep the Captain company. At least, that was how my mother, who cherished her silver, put it.

When the others had gone the Captain produced a stubby clay pipe and began to fill it. "Weel, laddie," he said, "an' hoo dae ye propose tae pass the Sabbath?"

"I've got a book of Bible stories," I said. "I could get you one, too, if you like."

"Na, na." He shook his head disapprovingly. "Us Holy Christians dinna haud wi' Bible stories. The Bible itsel' is good enough for us." His eyes moved questingly around the room. "A big braw hoose like this," he said with wonder, "an no' a drop o' whisky in sicht."

"We don't have whisky," I said. "It's bad for you."

"Aye, terrible!" He shuddered. "The demon rum."

"Except for medicine," I said. "For colds and like that."

He looked at me quickly. "That's jist why I mentioned it." He put his hand on his middle. "I'm sair distressed," he groaned. "Colly-wobbles, they ca' it. Fair torture an' nae cure for it but a drap or twa. Whaur does yer faither keep the whus—medicine?"

"In his room," I said. "But I'm not allowed to touch it."

"An' richtly so," said the Captain with approval. "Ye're ower young yet for that. But there's an exception tae everythin', so awa' ye like a good laddie an' get it for me."

I hesitated. Not even my mother would have mercy on

32

me if it were discovered that I had handled the whisky bottle. Then as the Captain groaned again fear for him seized me, and I got up and ran upstairs.

He was watching the doorway expectantly when I got back.

"Here." I twisted the cork from the almost full bottle and thrust it at him. "I'll get you a teaspoon."

"A teaspoon!" His mustache blew out. "Wad ye droon me? Naw, laddie, I'll jist tak' a wee nip an' see does it do wi' me." He lifted the bottle and poured down about a cupful. "Whoosh!" he exclaimed as he lowered it. "The real auld mountain dew."

I held out my hand. "I better put the bottle back now," I said nervously.

"Haud on." He drew it away from me. "We better wait a wee an' see does it ease me."

I stood waiting anxiously as he sat sucking contentedly at his pipe. It didn't seem to me now that he could be very sick, but he was a grown-up and grown-ups, I believed then, were above deceit or subterfuge. The minutes slid by and at last my mounting tension broke in speech:

"Is it not better yet?" I said.

"A wee thing, mebbe. I'll jist try another touch an' see does that do the trick." Again he tipped the bottle and drank at length.

Spots of colour were burning on his hairy cheeks now, and it seemed to me that his eyes had grown heavy. Then he must be sick, I thought, as I stood twirling the cork between my fingers. But sick or not, I had to get that bottle back to my father's room, and soon.

"Will I take the bottle now?" I said, when I had waited another five minutes.

He looked at me drowsily and then lifted the bottle and sucked at it again. A hoarse chuckle escaped him and he leaned back in his chair and closed his eyes. "I'll let ye ken," he said thickly. "When the bottle's empty."

Suddenly, with shock, I knew what his sickness was and saw how he had tricked me. My ingrained respect for him as an elder lost in anger and contempt, I snatched the bottle from his relaxed hand, corked it hurriedly, and ran from the room.

I was braced for anything from rage to drunken pleading

as I went back to the sitting room, but he was just as I had left him, except that he was fast asleep now, his bearded jaw hanging loose. Thankful to have the danger safely over, I got my book of Bible stories and sat down to wait for the others to come home.

The Captain was still sleeping peacefully when I heard the front door open. Voices murmured in the hall and then the sitting-room door opened and Grandma, followed by my parents, came in.

"Well, I never!" She stopped short and stared at the Captain, her heavy black brows lowering. "Did he not get his sleep last night?" She raised her voice. "Hamish!"

"Sh-h-h-h!" my father said, as the Captain slumbered on. "He's soul-searching."

Grandma threw him a glance of reproof and then went over to the Captain and shook his shoulder. "Hamish! Wake up, man!"

The Captain's eyes opened, dull and unfocussed, then as Grandma shook him again, they rose to her face. "Lizzie!" he said with a bleary grin. "Ma bonnie, bonnie lass. Gie's a kiss."

Grandma's breath drew in sharply, and for a little there was an awful silence.

"Drunk!" Grandma's voice came, heavy with shock and disgust. "The miserable gomeral! Drunk! And on the Lord's day!"

The Captain gave a wheezy chuckle, a hand feeling around in his chair. He looked up at me, scowling suddenly. "The bottle, laddie," he said, to my horror. "Did ye put it back?"

"Bottle?" my father said, and looked at me with wrath dawning in his eyes. "The bottle in my room?"

"Or ony ither bottle ye hae, Robert," said the Captain with a loose grin. "Me an' Lizzie's gaun tae hae a dram."

Grandma's face turned black with anger then. She seized a handful of the Captain's hair and shook him like a rag doll. "Och!" she raged. "You keeley blackguard! Get out of that chair! And out of this house! I'll put up with a lot for old time's sake, but I'll have no dealin's with drunkards and Sabbath-breakers. Away with you!"

Released, the Captain lurched to his feet, feeling tenderly at his mistreated scalp. Suddenly, he was considerably more

34

sober. "Noo, haud on, Lizzie," he said in an injured voice. "The laddie'll tell ye himsel'—I was taken poorly an'—"

"Away!" Her eyes blazing, Grandma pointed to the door. "Pack your bag, you low scunnersome creature, and get out of my sight!"

And as the Captain shuffled from the room, I wished unhappily that I might go with him. . . .

The hearing was held in the sitting room immediately after the Captain's departure. A guilty and fearful wretch, I stood with downcast eyes and explained the why and wherefore of my sinning. There was silence then, and I looked up and saw that my parents were having trouble keeping their faces straight. It dawned on me then that, actually, I had done them a favour and knew with relief that a leathering was unlikely.

"I have to admit, Dunc," my father said with an attempt at sternness, "that there are certain extenuating factors in all this. But the fact remains that you disobeyed me and therefore deserve a good sound thrashing."

Grandma wheeled on him, her grey eyes sparkling. "Better thrash yourself instead, Robert Mackinley," she snapped. "You, our natural protector, were totally blind to the evil of this stranger within your gate, but the Lord saw fit to open your eyes and the laddie was only the instrument in His hand."

GRANDMA
... and the Wee Pest

IF GRANDMA hadn't run out of pan drops (known on this side of the water as Scotch mints) it is highly improbable that the Wee Pest would ever have found her way into our lives. But Grandma would no more have sat through a sermon without a pan drop melting under her tongue than she would have walked to kirk in her bare feet; so there was nothing for her to do, this Saturday evening, but go into town and renew her supply. And I, with the frank opportunism of youth, tagged along with her.

Miss Turnbull, who kept the sweetie shop, was from Grandma's home town, Auchterfenty, so what with reminiscences and then a tour of the shop windows, it was more than an hour before we started back to the house; I with the fruits of my opportunism bulging my cheek, Grandma striding along beside me, lean, erect, grim and black-clad, a regular sergeant-major of a woman.

We had cleared the town and were walking up Kilburnie Road when from the darkness ahead of us a thin ululation of sound rose eerily in the warm Autumn air.

"Mercy on us!" said Grandma. "Like a soul in torment."

The wailing came steadily closer, and then, as we drew near a lamp post, we saw approaching us the familiar towering

36

figure of young Constable Angus Macphail, a struggling, vociferating bundle clasped in his arms.

"Gracious!" Grandma stopped short, barring his way. "Man, what are you doin' with that bairn?"

The Constable, his raw-boned face red and perspiring, managed to get a finger to his helmet. "It's no' what I'm doin' wi' the bairn, Mistress Guthrie," he said unhappily "it's what the bairn's doin' wi' me."

"But whose bairn is it?" said Grandma above the screaming of the baby.

The Constable shook his head dolefully. "My, a sair tragic thing, ma'am. Auld Colin Rennie's hoose jist burned doon an' him an' the bairn's mother in it."

I heard Grandma's breath draw in sharply, and felt a tingle of horror go through me. Colin Rennie's small truck garden lay in a hollow behind the golf course, a mile or so beyond my father's house, and the old fellow with his barrow of vegetables was a familiar sight in the neighbourhood. Until a month or two before, he had lived alone in his humble "but an' ben," and then a premature blast in the quarry at Fernie had taken the life of one James Dalry, and his widow, Colin's great-niece, had come with her infant daughter to find refuge with the old man.

"But, man alive," said Grandma, "if you were able to save the bairn, why not the others?"

"The bairn was ootside in a kind o' pram," explained the Constable. "Mistress Dalry aye kept her in the fresh air till Colin got done smokin' his pipe an' went tae bed."

"But what way could they not get out of the house?"

"Dear knows," said the Constable. "It'll be a day or two afore we get the bodies oot, for the lum and twa walls collapsed into the cellar, an' mebbe then we'll no' ken. Dr. Kerr was by an' telt me Colin's hairt was in bad shape an' that he mebbe drapped deid frae shock, but that doesna accoont for Mistress Dalry."

Grandma looked suddenly at the baby, still screaming at the top of its lungs. "What's the matter with the wee smout anyway?"

"Ach, jist hungry, I suppose."

"Hungry!" Grandma snorted and snatched the bundle from his arms. "That's not the way a bairn greets when it's

37

"It's no' what I'm doin' wi' the bairn, Mistress Guthrie . . ."

hungry." Her hand explored the infant's voluminous wrappings and I saw her nose wrinkle with distaste. "Fair droukit," she said. "You could sine her out like a dish clout." Then her hand came out holding an open safety pin, and the baby's shrieking died to a broken sobbing. "There's your hunger for you," she said acidly. "You great doited lump, could you not have found it for yourself?"

Grinning abashedly, the Constable extended his hands. "I'm a single man, ma'am, an' no' in the way o' bairns," he said. "But I'm rale obleeged tae ye. It was an awfu' uproar she was makin', the wee thing."

Grandma drew the baby away from him. "What are you goin' to do with her?" she demanded.

"I'm no' richt sure," said the Constable uncertainly. "I thocht mebbe I could find some woman tae look efter her till the next of kin turn up."

"Aye," said Grandma tartly, "and in the meantime the wee soul could perish of hunger and diaper rash. I'm takin' her home with me, Constable."

"Weel, there noo," said the Constable with obvious relief. "I'm sure it's mair than kind o' ye, Mistress Guthrie. But, ach, will it no' be a trauchle tae ye?"

"Aye, trauchle enough," said Grandma ungraciously. "As I ought to know, havin' raised six of my own. But I know the Lord's hand when I see it and I have no choice." She turned away. "Come, Duncan. It's high time this bairn was looked after."

My parents were in the sitting room when we reached the house. They glanced up as we came in and then straightened, staring.

"What on earth!" said my mother blankly. "Mamma, that isn't a baby?"

"It's not a monkey," said Grandma.

My mother looked expressively at my father. His mouth twitched.

"It can hardly be your own," he said solemnly.

Grandma gave him a glare of reproof and then told them of the tragedy.

My mother had lost colour. "Oh, how terrible!" she said in a stifled voice. "The poor, poor things!"

"Don't grieve for them," said Grandma. "They're with

the Lord now and safe forever." She went on and described our meeting with the Constable. "So I took charge of the wee thing," she finished. "You can see yourself it was the Lord's will."

My mother came over and looked at the baby, quiet now but wide awake. "What a pity!" she said. "Such a lovely wee girl, too." She looked up at Grandma. "But I don't know, Mamma," she said doubtfully. "It seems to me it would have been better to have let some woman with young children have her. We're not equipped here to take care of an infant."

"Havers!" said Grandma. "It's all in knowin' how." She marched across to my father and, to his obvious discomfiture, plumped the baby into his arms. "You hold her a minute, Robert, till I get my things off," she said. She turned. "You, Jessie, go out and tell Mary to put an egg on to coddle and then find me an old sheet or somethin' to rip up for diapers. . . . And you, Duncan." She took out her purse and handed me a shilling. "Away you back to town and get a baby's feeding bottle at the chemist's."

By the time I got back from town with the feeding bottle, the baby had finished her coddled egg and was ready for the warm milk Grandma had waiting. Absorbedly, I watched her fill the bottle and then laughed delightedly as I saw the little pink mouth snatch eagerly at the rubber nipple. I had no brothers or sisters and this business of caring for a baby was an entertaining novelty to me.

The bottle at last empty, the baby lay on Grandma's lap gurgling and kicking her little fat legs.

"Aye." Grandma looked down at her sourly. "You've got your belly full and that's all you care about. Nothin' to you, all the washin' and feedin' and bathin'—" She exclaimed suddenly and lifted the baby from her knees. "Ach, the wee pest! My good dress! Hand me another diaper, Jessie."

Smiling, my mother complied. "It's not the baby's fault, Mamma."

"Ach, I know it isn't her fault," said Grandma crossly. "But it's a sore trial, at my age, to be saddled with a bairn. It'll be no heartbreak, I can tell you, when her kin folk come for her."

Wherein, as it turned out, she was mistaken. . . .

40

The next day, Sunday, was grim. The baby, who had been installed in a makeshift crib in Grandma's room, had wakened at midnight and from then until morning had kept Grandma in what she called a "perfect cafuffle." The result was that the old lady, with less than two hours sleep, was so irritable and crabbed that we were almost afraid to speak to her. Nor was her disposition improved by the fact that because of the baby she would have to stay home from kirk. My mother, knowing how much kirk meant to her, offered to stay with the baby for one of the services, but Grandma refused. It was her responsibility she said, placed on her by the Lord, and she would shoulder it herself.

At noon on Monday I came home from school for lunch and was waiting in the sitting room with my parents and Grandma, when the doorbell in the kitchen clanged. A minute later the sitting-room door opened and the maid put her head in.

"A Mr. and Mrs. Cochran," she whispered. "They've come tae tak the bairn."

There was an instant of silence, then Grandma rose, and I wondered at the strained tightness of her face. "Send them in, Mary," she said, and was still standing there when the door opened again.

The couple who walked into the room appeared to be in their late thirties, an oddly assorted pair. He was small, scrawny, shabby, with pale blue eyes that peered out knowingly from under wisps of sandy eyebrows; she was large, obese, with straggling black hair and little suspicious black eyes embedded like currants in the doughy masses of her sallow face.

The little man addressed himself to Grandma. "Would you be Mistress Guthrie?"

"I am," said Grandma coldly. "And this is my good son, and daughter and grandson. Will you be seated?"

Unlike his wife, who chose to ignore us, Mr. Cochran returned my parents' greetings and sat down beside her on the sofa.

"An awfu' business," he said, shaking his head. "Ma poor sister! First her man an' noo hersel'. They still havena got the bodies oot, they tell me."

"So I understand," said Grandma. "You've come for the bairn, of course?"

41

"I suppose so." There was a notable lack of enthusiasm in Mr. Cochran's voice. "It was guid o' ye tae tak her in."

The woman spoke for the first time. "Did his sister leave any money?"

Grandma's eyes glinted in their deep sockets. "If she did it went up with the house."

"What aboot Colin? Did he have anythin' in the bank?"

"I doubt it," said Grandma curtly. "But you could inquire."

"What aboot insurance? Or stocks? At his age he must have had somethin' put by."

Open distaste appeared in Grandma's face. "I know nothin' whatever about his affairs, but I might say it seems to me you're gey taken up with that side of it."

The woman looked up at her sullenly. "What for no'? If there's anythin' coming to us we want it."

"Anythin' comin' to you!" Grandma's eyes blazed at her. "You're gettin' a bonnie wee bairn, are you not? Is that not enough?"

The woman's narrow mouth twisted. "Bairn! I hae a' the bairns I want."

"Then what are you here for?" demanded Grandma. "The bairn's all you're goin' to get. There's little doubt that everythin' Colin and your good sister owned was lost in the fire—barrin' maybe a few garden tools."

The woman's eyes were bright with anger. "If that's the way of it," she said spitefully, "the bairn'll go to an orphanage."

"Orphanage!" Grandma gasped the word. "You cold heartless wretch! You'd do a thing like that to the poor wee soul?"

"Ach, she doesna mean it," Mr. Cochran said hastily. "But it's true enough—we can ill afford tae feed another wean. If we could find a good hame for her we'd be glad tae let her go."

Grandma was silent, her eyes on his face but not seeing it. "All right," she said suddenly. "You've found your good home—I'll keep the bairn myself. If I can raise six I can raise another."

My mother gasped and straightened abruptly in her chair. "But, Mamma—"

42

"Hold your tongue, Jessie!" snapped Grandma. "Not a word out of you!"

My mother looked appealingly at my father. He shook his head, and biting her lip she settled back in the chair.

Mr. Cochran's pale eyes were squinting up at Grandma. "I meant," he said, "we'd be glad tae let her go if it was made worth oor while."

"Aye," Grandma nodded slowly. "I might have known it. And how much would be worth your while?"

Mr. Cochran hesitated, eyeing his wife sidewise. She spoke for him.

"Twenty pounds."

Grandma snorted. "Do you see any green in my eye? I'll give you five."

"Well, fifteen."

"Five," said Grandma. "And the price of your fares to wherever you came from. My last offer. I'm willin' to keep the bairn but I've no mind to be robbed."

Mr. and Mrs. Cochran eyed each other in silent communion.

"All richt," said Mr. Cochran, "we'll tak it—though it's little enough. Dae ye have it in cash?"

"I have," said Grandma dryly. "But it's not that simple." She looked over at my father. "Who's your lawyer, Robert?"

"Currie, Duncan & Currie."

Grandma turned to the Cochrans. "Tomorrow at ten I'll meet you at the office of Currie, Duncan & Currie in town and we'll have the thing done legally."

"But that means we'll hae tae stay here till the morn," Mr. Cochran protested.

"I'll allow you ten shillin's for expenses," said Grandma. She sniffed. "And at that you'll make money on me, I haven't a doubt."

Through all this my mother had been sitting simmering. The instant the door closed on the Cochrans she shot to her feet. "Good gracious, Mamma! What on earth are you think- ing of? You can't go through with this. It's—it's insane."

"That'll be enough, Jessie," said Grandma sternly. "I know well what I'm thinkin' of. The Lord has put this bairn in my arms and I can't betray His trust."

43

"But to adopt it, Mamma! Surely it wasn't necessary to go that far?"

"It was necessary to do whatever was best for the bairn, and the best was to get her forever out of the clutches of that scunnersome pair of rogues."

"All right, Mamma, it was. But why try to bring her up? She's a lovely baby and you'd have no trouble finding some reliable couple to take her off your hands."

"No doubt, Jessie. But when I sign these papers tomorrow the bairn'll be mine, legally and in the eyes of the Lord, and I'll never hand any bairn of mine over to strangers."

"Oh-h-h!" My mother swung around and looked beseechingly at my father. He raised his eyebrows plaintively.

"Why look at me, Jess? If your mother wants to tie herself down with a baby, there's nothing I can do to stop her. She knows what it'll mean—work and worry and sleepless nights, maybe broken health. She knows it's bad for a bairn to move it around and that she'll have to stay close to home, not able to visit her children or even go to kirk—"

"Save your breath, Robert," snapped Grandma. "Your wife's proddin' you on, but you know as well as I do you can't move me. This is the Lord's work I'm undertakin'." And then, as a wail of distress came from upstairs, her face darkened. "Ach, the perfect wee pest!" she complained. "Will you listen to her! And I haven't had my lunch yet. . . ."

That afternoon after school I hurried straight home. The baby was due a feeding at four o'clock and I wanted to witness at least part of this fascinating proceeding. I found her in the sitting room on Grandma's knee, the bottle already half gone, a tiny fist clutching at Grandma's sinewy wrist, and stood watching the little round cheeks pump in and out. And then, too soon, the bottle was empty and Grandma got up wearily and carried her off to bed.

In less than five minutes Grandma came back, and my mother looked up from her crocheting.

"Asleep already?"

"Aye," said Grandma dourly and dropped heavily down on a chair. "Which means that wee pest'll have me up all night, I suppose."

At this moment the doorbell jangled, and we heard Mary walk out through the hall. A woman's voice came, high-pitched

44

and urgent, and then our door opened and a wild-eyed distraught girl pushed past Mary into the room. With amazement, I recognized her.

"Ma baby!" she cried. "Whaur's ma wee Teeny?"

Grandma and my mother were staring at her blankly.

"It's Mrs. Dalry, Grandma!" I said excitedly. "You know —the baby's mother."

Grandma got up slowly, disbelief on her face. "Havers, laddie! It can't be."

"But I am!" cried the girl. "Is my wee Teeny safe?"

"Well, I never!" said Grandma. "You poor creature, of course she is. Upstairs fast asleep and doin' fine."

"Oh, thank God!" Mrs. Dalry sank down on a chair. "I was sae feared for her. I'm a stranger in these parts an' I didna ken what tae expect."

"But where have you been, lassie?" said Grandma. "It's two days since the fire."

"Ower in Arran. I heard of a body who wanted a housekeeper. Uncle Colin was sae fond o' Teeny an' sae handy wi' her, so I left him tae look after her an' took the late boat on Saturday tae Lamlash. I got the job, too, an' permission tae bring Teeny with me, but when I got back tae the pier the last boat had gone an' there wasna another till this afternoon. An' then when I got here an' they told me—" She broke off, her mouth trembling.

"Aye, poor lassie," said Grandma. "I can imagine it. But there—we'll have a cup of tea and then—"

"But I canna wait, Mrs. Guthrie. I've got to go right back, an' the last boat leaves in half an hour. I'll be here for Uncle Colin's funeral, though, when—when—"

"Aye, I understand," said Grandma. "Don't think about it." She turned to my mother. "Jessie, while I'm gettin' the bairn's things together, run up and bring her down."

Five minutes later Mrs. Dalry stood in the hall ready to leave, the baby, still asleep, cradled in her arms; a bundle containing spare diapers and the feeding bottle, dangling from a finger.

Grandma had been poking in her purse. "And you better take this," she said gruffly. "There'll be things to buy for the wee one and for yourself."

Mrs. Dalry glanced down at the folded note Grandma

45

had tucked in her hand. "Oh, ye shouldna!" she protested. "Five pounds! After a' yer kindness."

"Ach, whist, lassie!" said Grandma testily. "No need of goin' on about it. Just see you take good care of the bairn, for I was very nearly her mother."

"Oh, I will, Mrs. Guthrie," the girl said. "And I thank ye frae the bottom o' ma hairt."

The door closed on Mrs. Dalry, and Grandma and my mother stood watching through the glass panel as she hurried down the path.

"Well," my mother said with relief in her voice, "this has all turned out better than I would have dared hope for."

"It has turned out," said Grandma, "exactly the way the Lord intended, and I'm happy that He trusted me to serve His ends."

My mother looked around at her curiously. "You don't sound very happy, Mamma. In fact, you almost sound—"

"Ach, don't blether, lassie!" snapped Grandma, and turned quickly away. "Dreigh wee pest—I'll be able to get some sleep tonight."

But as she passed me on her way to the stairway, I saw with wonder that her grey eyes had filled with tears.

GRANDMA
. . . and the Plum Tree

THE PLUM TREE stood in Grandma's back garden. It had been growing there for years when, after my grandfather's death, she bought and moved into the cottage. It was a fine big tree, healthy and well-grown, and every spring, when it simply exploded into bloom, an arresting and eye-filling sight.

But it had one shortcoming — it never bore any fruit worth mentioning.

Grandma never complained about that, however. The picture it made every spring, she always said, was reward enough for the little care it got; and if the Lord saw fit to withhold its bearing, who was she to question His designs? Not, from some points of view, a very practical attitude, perhaps, but Grandma was more devout than horticultural minded.

So there it grew, a familiar sight of my boyhood, though not markedly different from a million others of its kind all over Scotland. And yet, as I see it now, like no other tree anywhere in the world. . . .

I was eleven that spring and a convalescent from scarlet fever when I went to Ardrach to spend a few days with Grandma. Aunt Hetty, Grandma's youngest, had left now to take up nursing and the old lady was alone. But as she met me at the station there was nothing in her lean grim face to tell of her pleasure at seeing me or of how welcome I was in

*"Foosh!" a voice said behind us. "Hae ye never
been in an art gallery?"*

her aloneness. Just the same, I knew the pleasure was there
and recognized the brisk little cuffing movement with which
she straightened my rumpled forelock for the caress it actually
was. And, strange though it may seem, I was as happy to be
with her as she was to have me.

At the cottage, she fed me, gleaned what few scraps of
news about home I was able to give her, and then, with charac-
teristic abruptness, picked up a half-filled laundry basket and
marched out the back door. Left to myself, I looked with
contentment around the small cheery kitchen, with its wide tiled
range and row of burnished copper pots; but I was too young
to sit still for long and, presently, I got up and followed her
into the bright spring sunlight.

I found her at the clothes line in the back garden, her
basket nearly empty. The air was full of the smell of growing
things and the plum tree, I saw with a lift of pleasure, was
resplendent in billowing masses of bloom.

I was still looking up at it with the rapt, marvelling eyes

48

of childhood when Grandma, having pegged her last piece of wash, came over to my side.

"Aye, a bonnie, bonnie sight," she said with reverence in her voice. "Only the Lord, Duncan, could make a thing so pleasin' to the eye."

"Foosh!" a voice said behind us. "Hae ye never been in an art gallery, mem?"

I glanced around. Above the low stone wall that divided Grandma's back garden from the property next door, I saw the torso of a stout man of about sixty, clean-shaven and with the butt of a cigar screwed in to the corner of his mouth, and recognized Mr. Wallace Bruce Calhoun. Mr. Calhoun, a retired plumber, had moved into the house next door during the winter. He was a bachelor, with a predilection for cigars and fancy waistcoats, tastes that Grandma viewed with no more than a mildly jaundiced eye; but he was also a prideful and aggressive scoffer at what he described as "a' this religious jookery-pookery," and Grandma, much to his vexation, treated him with a consistent cold contempt.

Grandma, too, had turned her eyes glinting along her beak of a nose. "Certainly, sir, I've been in an art gallery," she said coldly. "What about it?"

"Ye need ask me?" said Mr. Calhoun with over-affected surprise. "Did ye no' see anythin' there pleasin' to the eye?"

"I did so. But nothin' to compare with this tree."

"Ach!" Mr. Calhoun removed his cigar and spat expressively. "As if there was onythin' patent aboot that tree or any ither tree. I could grow as good a wan mysel' wi' jist my least wee bit touch."

"Could you, now?" said Grandma dryly. " 'The tongue is a little member and boasteth great things.' "

Mr. Calhoun's round face coloured angrily. "Ye think I'm boastin', dae ye? Well, jist you haud on an' I'll show ye a tree every bit as good as yer ain." He sneered. "Aye, an' I'll no' need the Lord tae help me, either."

Grandma stooped swiftly and picked up her basket. "You're a fool, sir!" she snapped. "A blind fool. Without the Lord's help you couldn't even crook your finger." She wheeled away from him. "Come, Duncan."

But fool though Mr. Calhoun may have been, he wasn't without enterprise; for it was only a day or two later, while I

49

was playing in the back garden, that I saw him emerge from his house with a small tree across his shoulder and a spade in his hand.

"Aye, tak a good look," he said sourly, as he caught sight of me. "Then awa' in an' tell your grannie I'm plantin' a plum tree in my kale yard."

I watched him while he dropped the tree and began to dig and then turned and went into the house. Grandma was in the kitchen, making scones for tea.

"Mr. Calhoun's got a plum tree," I said.

"A plum tree?"

"A wee one," I explained, and held my hand above my head. "He's diggin' a hole for it."

Grandma drew her griddle to the back of the range and went out to the scullery behind the kitchen. Its window looked out across the wash house roof on both gardens and we had a clear view of Mr. Calhoun as he went about his planting. Already he had dug the hole and, holding the tree in place, was scuffing the earth around its roots with his foot. This done, he patted it down with the spade and then stood back and admired his handiwork.

Grandma sniffed. "Glaikit creature! A bonnie lookin' plum tree it'll be."

"Why, Grandma?" I said.

"Because he's doin' it wrong. He should have made a glaur with earth an' water to pack around its roots. An' he hasn't used a speck of manure to give it a start."

"Why don't you tell him, Grandma?"

"Tell him!" She turned, her eyes snapping. "Am I daft? Solomon knew his kind well: 'Fools despise wisdom and instruction,' and 'The instruction of fools is folly.' Tell him, indeed! I wouldn't waste my breath."

But though she refused to advise Mr. Calhoun, I could see during the next forty-eight hours that she was none the less concerned for the tree. And with reason. Obviously, it was dying, its few tender leaves withering and turning brown. If something wasn't done for it, and soon, it was doomed.

On the afternoon of the third day I was in the back garden when Mr. Calhoun came strolling out from his house. With a curt nod he went past me to the young plum tree and stood looking at it.

50

"Humph!" He removed his cigar and spat. "Kind o' peely-wally looking, the thing."

"Grandma says it's goin' to die," I told him.

He scowled. "Och, did she, now? I suppose the Lord told her?"

"No," I said. "Because you didn't plant it right."

"Plant it right!" He laughed wheezily. "As if ye could plant it wrong! It came oot o' the earth an' went back tae the earth, an' a' it needs is time. Jist tell that tae the ould blether, my young cockalorum."

At tea-time I reported the conversation to Grandma, and saw her heavy brows draw down over her eyes.

"The gomeral!" she said with contempt. " 'Wise in his own conceit.' " She was silent for a little, her grey eyes thoughtful, and then looked across at me. "Duncan, when you've done your tea you might take a pail along the road an' see can you scrape me up some horse droppin's."

I looked at her with astonishment. "What for, Grandma?"

"For the tree, laddie."

"But why?" I said blankly. "It's not your tree."

"No." A glow came into her eyes. "It's not my tree, laddie; it's the Lord's tree, an' just as much His creature as you an' me."

"But Mr. Calhoun'll be vexed if you do anythin' to it."

She grunted. "Mr. Calhoun'll know nothin' about it. He always takes his bit daunder of an evenin', an' that'll be my chance to do the Lord's work."

"But if the tree lives," I objected, "Mr. Calhoun'll think it was his own doin'."

"Aye." A shadow passed across her face. "A' he'll gloat, the creature, I haven't a doubt. But there—the Lord'll know the truth."

It seemed to me that Mr. Calhoun would never set out for his stroll that evening, but at last, just as dusk was falling, he emerged from his house, a fresh cigar rammed in the corner of his mouth, and strutted off along the roadway.

Grandma had everything ready — a newspaper, a trowel, a pail of water, the pailful of manure, and even a wooden box to help her over the wall. Three minutes after Mr. Calhoun's departure we were kneeling by the young plum tree.

With the trowel Grandma dug the earth away from the

51

tree's roots and piled it on the newspaper. When they were free I lifted it clear and watched her make a mud puddle in the bottom of the hole. I put the tree back and steadied it while she sprinkled alternate layers of earth and manure around its roots until the hole was almost full. Then she dumped the rest of the water in and, when it had soaked down, filled the hole with dry earth from the newspaper and patted it flat. You could hardly tell then that the tree had been disturbed.

"There!" she said with satisfaction, as she rose. "That's all a body can do for the poor wee thing. Whether it lives or dies now rests with the Lord."

Unfortunately I had to go home the next day, so, although I heard from Grandma that the tree had lived, it wasn't until the summer when, as always, I went to stay with her that I was able to see what progress it had made. And then, with a kind of awe, I saw the new leaves and shoots it had put forth and knew that indeed Grandma had been working with the Lord.

And now, the Lord's work done, this should have been the end of the matter. But there was still the devil to be reckoned with.

Indirectly, I was the cause of the scene that took place between Grandma and Mr. Calhoun the following spring. I had just arrived to spend a weekend with her and was sitting in the kitchen, watching her iron, when I remembered our adventure of the spring before.

"How's Mr. Calhoun's plum tree, Grandma?" I said.

"Oh, aye!" She looked at me, a little gleam in her eyes. "You haven't seen it, have you?" She put her iron back on the range top and crooked a finger at me. "Come," she said, and led the way to the door.

I followed her down the back steps and along the side of the wash house. As we cleared it she stopped suddenly, and I saw that Mr. Calhoun was pacing his garden, the inevitable cigar in his mouth. For a little Grandma hesitated, and I guessed that since the spring before she had been careful to give him no chance to gloat about the tree. Then I saw her face stiffen and she continued on her way.

As we aproached him, Mr. Calhoun stopped his pacing and stood watching us expectantly, but Grandma passed him without so much as a glance, and I saw his mouth twist in a sneer. Then as Grandma came to a stop near the bottom of the garden my eyes fell on the young plum tree across the wall and I felt a tingle of surprise and pleasure. The new growth was only to be expected, but I was quite unprepared for the masses of bloom that covered it.

"By gum!" I said. "You fixed it, Grandma."

She looked down at me, dour and grim, but with the gleam back in her eyes. "The Lord fixed it, Duncan. The wee thing has done real well, has it not?"

"Champion," I said.

"Weel, I'm glad tae hear ye admit it," Mr. Calhoun's voice said sourly from our right.

I turned quickly, sure that he had heard me, but his next words brought reassurance.

"Ye didna ken I had a green thumb, did ye, mem?" he said jeeringly.

Grandma eyed him with cold disfavour. "It's of not the slightest interest to me, sir, what kind of a thumb you have."

Mr. Calhoun's face darkened. "Aye, ye're such a superior body, wi' your way o' it. But for a' yer superiority, ye were wrong aboot the tree. I had planted it wrong, ye telt the laddie there, an' it was gaun tae die." His voice rose in triumph. "But it didna die, did it? Did it?"

"No, it didn't," snapped Grandma. "But it's no thanks to you."

"Is that a fact?" Mr. Calhoun arched his eyebrows insolently. "Then wha's it thanks tae?"

"To the Lord, mostly."

"Och aye, the Lord." He grinned derisively. "The Lord dug the hole for it, no' me."

The irreverence brought a gasp from Grandma. "You blasphemous, ill-bred gomeral, you had nothin' to do with it!" she said furiously, stung out of discretion. "You left it there to die, but I watered it an' fertilized it an' the Lord saw fit then to give it back its life."

Mr. Calhoun removed his cigar, staring. "You what?" he said blankly.

"You heard me," said Grandma. "As my grandson here can tell you, I dug it out of the dry fushionless earth an' planted it properly." She gave a snort of contempt. "You an' your green thumb!"

Mr. Calhoun lifted his cigar suddenly and dashed it to the ground, his face crimson with chagrin. "Officious auld carlin!" he snarled. "Ye think ye did a great stroke, dae ye, trespassin' on my property an' interferin' wi' my affairs? Weel, by the holy Moses, I'll show ye! I'll show ye!" His face contorted with rage, he rushed at the young tree and threw his weight against it, thrusting and tearing at it. Its slender bole bent to and fro helplessly in his grasp, and then there was a tearing crack and it buckled in the middle. Not satisfied yet, however, he twisted it around and around until the fibres parted and he held the flowering top in his hands. "There!" he raged, and trampled it into the ground. "There's yer tree that you an' the Lord had sich a conceit o'!"

I glanced up at Grandma and saw that her eyes were blazing in a colorless face. Without speaking, she went over slowly to the wall and stopped, a dark, menacing, silent figure.

I don't know what Mr. Calhoun saw in her face, but his angry flush ebbed away and I saw something like apprehension dawn in his eyes. "What are ye glowerin' at?" he blustered feebly. "It was my ain tree, was it no?"

"Aye, it was your own tree." Grandma's voice was hardly more than a whisper. "But, like Satan himself, you have destroyed without reason, an' you'll surely answer to the Lord for it." She turned her back on him. "Come, Duncan."

I followed her into the house. In the kitchen she stood looking out the window, and when, at last, she turned I saw that her eyes were moist.

"I'm awfully sorry, Grandma," I offered. "He's a dirty rotter."

She shook her head. "Don't be sorry for me, laddie. It was my own doin', my own sinful pride. I allowed myself to boast to him about what I'd done, not mindin' what the Book tells us: 'Him that hath an high look and a proud heart will not I suffer.' Now the Lord has punished me."

Here, it would seem, my story should end, but the devil having done his worst, there is still a last brief scene that rests, very properly, with the Lord.

That summer when school closed I went back to Ardrach to stay with Grandma. I had been there a day or two when, while playing in the back garden one afternoon, I happened to glance up into the plum tree. For a little I stood motionless, staring, and then turned and ran into the house. Grandma was in the sitting room, busy with her endless knitting.

"The plum tree, Grandma!" I cried. "You didn't tell me."

"What are you haverin' about?" She looked at me dourly over stilled fingers. "Tell you what?"

I realized then that she hadn't known, any more than I had.

"I've got a surprise for you," I said, and tugged at her sleeve. "Come on, Grandma. Let me show you."

"Ach, you're a perfect wee pest," she complained. But she laid aside her knitting, and I led her out to the plum tree and pointed upward. Under its foliage every branch and twig was lined with small green plums, hundreds of them, bushels of them.

Grandma was silent for a little, and then I heard her breath come out in a kind of sigh. "The Lord's doin'!" she said with wonder and exaltation in her voice. "The Lord's unfailin' justice. He punished me for my pride, but I had done His work nevertheless and now this is my reward."

And, of course, I believed her.

And, now that I'm nearly as old as Grandma was then, I still believe her. For, certainly, there is no finer example of God's handiwork than the miracle of cross-pollination between two trees.

GRANDMA
. . . and the Tappit Hen

GRANDMA, as a rule, made a point of being back from her afternoon "daunder" in time for tea, but this evening she was late and we had nearly finished before she joined us.

"Really, Mamma," my mother said, as she took the cosy from the teapot, "you're unwise, surely, to walk so far. After all, you're not a young woman any more."

"Havers, Jessie!" Grandma, who was in a definitely bad humour about something, turned offended grey eyes on her. "If I was a blubbery wee soft puddin' of a thing like you, you'd do well to worry, but the Lord, praise be, has spared me my figure and I'll walk the legs off you any day of the week."

I saw my father's mouth twitch. Grandma's figure was of the ramrod variety—a tough, resilient, tempered ramrod.

"Forbye," added Grandma, "I wasn't walkin'."

"Oh?" A little flushed at the indelicate reference to her lower limbs, my mother handed her her tea. "Where were you, Mamma?"

Grandma stirred her tea in silence for a little. "I was at a roup," she said at last, grudgingly.

"A roup? Who was having a roup?"

"A Mrs. Macleod—in that wee brick house just off the esplanade near town. A sorry case, poor soul—left alone in the world with barely enough to buy her bread and havin' to auction off everythin' and move into a single room."

"Yes, a great pity," my mother said abstractedly, anxious eyes on Grandma's face. "But, Mamma, you didn't buy anything?"

"Aye, I bought somethin'," said Grandma morosely. "But I had no such intention."

My parents exchanged puzzled glances.

"What do you mean, Mamma?" my mother said.

"Ach!" Grandma moved her shoulders angrily. "It vexed me to see the poor feckless old body sittin' there, lettin' them snap up her bit things for next to nothin', so I began to bid them up, hopin' to get her better prices. It worked fine, too. Then this box of dishes came up—just a lot of trash—and did not this great dreigh lump of a man I was biddin' against let them go to me at five shillin's!"

A soft grunt escaped my father, and I saw his face turn crimson with suppressed laughter.

Grandma, fortunately, was unconscious of his merriment. "And to make matters worse," she complained bitterly, "did I not have to give a carter another shillin' to bring them here!"

My mother glanced at my father, then quickly away. "Oh, well," she said with a tremor in her voice. "No doubt they'll come in handy for bazaars and rummage sales."

We were rising from the table when the carter arrived with the box of dishes and, at Grandma's bidding, I showed him out to the storeroom at the back of the house. I went back to the sitting room and had just sat down when the bell in the kitchen rang. A moment or two later Mary Strachan, the maid, came in and closed the door.

"It's Fergus Rankin, the second-hand dealer," she said with distaste. "He wants to see you, Mrs. Guthrie."

"Well, he's got a good cheek," my mother said. "Coming to the front door."

"Not at all, Jess," my father said solemnly. "Social call, you know."

Grandma glared at him and then turned to Mary. "Send him in, Mary."

The individual who presently stood before us was large, fat, greasy of person, fawning of manner and evasive of eye. Clutching the remains of a bowler hat with grimy fingers, he singled Grandma out with what can be described only as a fond smile.

"Ye'll forgie this intrusion, I hope, Mistress Guthrie," he said. "But I wanted a word wi' ye."

"Well?"

Mr. Rankin glanced furtively at my parents. "It was aboot a box o' dishes ye bocht this efternoon at Mistress Macleod's roup."

"Well?"

"I was wonderin' would ye care tae sell them, Mistress Guthrie?"

"Why? What's your interest in them?"

Mr. Rankin's eyes slid away from her face. "I'll tell ye," he said. "I had it in mind tae be at the roup, but I had tae tak a run up tae Gourock first an' when I got back the roup was ower. But I saw there the box o' dishes ye bocht an' I minded then that the wife's in sair need o' some delft for the hoose. If ye're willin' I'll gie ye a shillin' more'n they cost ye."

"Will you, now?" Grandma's eyes narrowed cannily. "Then maybe I'd better keep them."

"Ach, that's no wiselike, Mistress Guthrie," protested Mr. Rankin. "They're no' good enough for the likes o' you. Tell ye what I'll dae—I'll gie ye ten shillin' for the lot. Double your money."

Grandma shook her head firmly. "No, thank you. They're not for sale."

Mr. Rankin had lost his smile.

"My certes!" he complained. "Ye're a hard bargainer. A poond, then. I'm a fool tae dae it, but I'll gie ye a poond."

Grandma rose majestically and rang the bell. "I told you, sir, they're not for sale. I wish you good-evening."

"Now, wait a wee, Mistress Guthrie—"

"Not a word, sir!" Grandma turned to Mary, who had appeared with suspicious promptness. "Show Mr. Rankin out, Mary."

"Good gracious, Mamma!" my mother said, as the door closed. "Why on earth didn't you let him have them?"

Grandma turned brooding eyes on her. "My, but you're the gullible one, Jessie. It's the Lord's mercy you have a man to look after you. Can you not see that if they're worth a pound of that rascal's money, they're probably worth more?"

58

"Right enough," my father said, and got up. "Maybe we'd better go out and have a look at them."

In the storeroom my father lit the gas, and we stood looking down at the box of dishes. They were a sorry looking collection — plates, saucers, cups, egg-cups, jugs and other odds and ends, most of them cracked or chipped, the detritus of years of housekeeping. Then my father stooped suddenly and from a corner of the box lifted a vessel of some dull grey metal, about a foot high and with a hinged lid that fitted neatly over its pouring lip.

"Well!" he said. "A tappit hen! This'll be what he was after."

"A what?" said Grandma.

"A tappit hen—a kind of flagon they used in Scotland a century or two ago. See?"

He held it sidewise to us, and I saw then the resemblance to a tappit (or crested) bird—the covered pouring lid for its beak, the knob on the lid for its crest.

But Grandma was not impressed. "A bonnie lookin' thing, I'm sure," she said. "What's it made of?"

"Pewter."

"Pewter!" She sniffed. "Poor stuff. I wouldn't have it in my house."

"Maybe not," my father said. "But some of the finest pewterware in museums today was made in Scotland in the seventeenth century, and though I don't pretend to be an authority on the subject, I have a notion that this thing is valuable. Certainly our friend Rankin seemed to think so."

"Well, there!" With wonder I heard the chagrin in Grandma's voice. "Faithless gomeral that I am — grievin' over my six shillin's instead of trustin' the Lord. I should have known He would reward me for tryin' to help that poor old creature."

"Why, Mamma!" my mother said with shock. "You're surely not thinking of keeping it?"

"Indeed I am, Jessie. Just that."

"But you can't!" gasped my mother. "Rankin knows about it and it would be bound to get out what you'd done. You've simply got to give it back."

Grandma's face was like a stone. "I'll not give it back.

59

It's mine as the Lord intended. But I can see his whole purpose now, and I know what I have to do."

My mother made a little gesture of despair and swung around to my father. "Robert!"

My father was looking at Grandma, his eyes puzzled. "You don't really mean it—that you're going to keep it?"

"I most certainly do, Robert."

"But that isn't right," my father said. "You know yourself it isn't. Legally it may be yours, but morally you have no right to keep it."

Anger glinted in Grandma's grey eyes. "Robert Mackinley, have you ever known me to do a dishonest thing?"

"No," my father said. "And never expect to. It's just that I don't understand how you can justify keeping it."

"No, Robert. Because you're not seein' the thing with the Lord's eyes." She took the tappit hen from him and tucked it under her arm. "But you needn't fash yourselves, either of you. I'll keep this thing but it'll be to Mrs. Macleod's profit, to my own profit, to the confusion of a rogue and to the shame of nobody."

And Grandma wheeled around and marched from the storeroom.

About ten the next morning, a Saturday, I was in the lower hall when Grandma came down the stairway. She was dressed in her Sabbath best, her handbag on her wrist, a neat package under her arm. As she paused to put on her gloves my mother came hurrying out of the sitting room.

"Why Mamma!" she exclaimed. "Where are you going?"

"Glasgow," said Grandma. "On the 10.31. I'll be back this afternoon."

"But why, Mamma? What for?"

Grandma finished drawing on her gloves. "On the Lord's business," she said, and strode to the door.

When my father came home at lunch-time my mother lost no time in telling him of Grandma's mysterious behaviour. "What do you suppose she's up to?" she said worriedly. "I'm sure that was the tappit hen she had under her arm."

My father shook his head. "Dear knows, Jess. But I wouldn't worry, if I were you."

"But I do worry," my mother said. "She does such—such peculiar things."

60

"I'll keep this thing, but it'll be to Mrs. Macleod's profit, to my own profit, to the confusion of a rogue and to the shame of nobody."

My father grinned. "You've got it wrong, lass. She does normal things but in such a peculiar way. A good woman, though, your mother . . ."

Around three that afternoon I was going through the motions of raking the gravel path, a victim of parental tyranny, when the front gate creaked and I saw Grandma bearing down on me. As she came abreast of me, erect and grim, she stopped abruptly, opened her handbag, thrust a small paper bag at me, cuffed me on the ear and in unbroken silence went on into the house. The neat package I noticed was still under her arm.

My labours lightened by the cinnamon bull's-eye melting in my cheek, I was back at my raking when again the gate creaked. This time it was a little old lady with a sweet innocent face and white hair peeping from under her plain black bonnet. Almost timorously she came toward me and stopped.

"I'm looking for a Mrs. Guthrie," she said apologetically. "This is the right house, is it not?"

"Yes." Glad of an excuse to spare my back, I dropped the rake. "Come in and I'll tell her you're here."

"Thank you, laddie. I'm sure you're very kind. The name's Macleod—Mrs. Macleod."

Filled suddenly with a sense of events impending, I led the way up the front steps and into the hall. The sitting room door was open and I saw that Grandma had changed and was there with my parents.

"Grandma," I said, "there's a lady here to see you. A Mrs. Macleod."

My mother gave a little dismayed gasp, and a three-second silence followed. Then Grandma rose and came over to the door. Her face, as always, was hard and dour, yet I knew somehow that she was pleased.

"How do you do, Mrs. Macleod?" she said, confirming my impression. "I'm glad to see you. Come away in and sit down."

While she went about introducing Mrs. Macleod to my parents and getting her seated, I slipped into the room and sat down on a straight chair by the door, hoping I wouldn't be noticed.

Introductions over, there was a little silence, then Mrs. Macleod ventured to suggest that it was a nice day, and my mother said yes, wasn't it, especially for this time of the year, and then there was another silence.

Grandma broke it. "Well, Mrs. Macleod," she said, with something like anticipation in her voice. "What can I do for you?"

Mrs. Macleod clasped and unclasped small work-worn hands. "It was about the box of dishes you bought," she said with difficulty. "There was an old pewter jug among them, one that came to me through my husband's family. I never cared for it, it was so useless and hard to keep polished, and I had no idea it was worth anythin'. Then this mornin' Mr. Rankin, the second-hand dealer, dropped by. I'm sure I don't know what you'll think of me, suggestin' such a thing, but he told me if I could get it back from you, he might give me as much as ten shillin's for it."

"Aye," said Grandma with grim satisfaction, and looked meaningly at my father. "I jaloused that would be his next move. Which is one reason I made up my mind to keep it."

"But Mamma," my mother said quickly, "you'll give it back now?"

"I will not," said Grandma. She turned back to the old lady. "This mornin', Mrs. Macleod, I took your pewter jug to a cousin of mine, an antique dealer in Glasgow. He told me it was what they call a tappit hen, made here in Scotland about the year 1670, and offered to buy it."

"Dear me!" said Mrs. Macleod. "Fancy people wantin' to pay out good money for a shabby old thing like that."

"You may well say it," agreed Grandma. "But here's the question, Mrs. Macleod: Would you rather have your tappit hen or the twenty-five guineas he offered me for it?"

The innocent old face went blank with incredulity. "Twenty . . . five . . . guineas!"

"Less my expenses, of course," said Grandma.

"But I — I can hardly dare believe it," said Mrs. Macleod bewilderedly.

"Are you sure the poor fella didn't make a mistake — such a lot of money?"

Grandma grunted. "Catch Cousin Willie makin' a mistake!" She took her handbag from the table. "My railway fare was three-and-six and another tuppence for trams — three-and-eight." She closed one eye. "See now — that leaves

63

me owin' you twenty-six pounds, one shillin' and fourpence." She counted the money into Mrs. Macleod's lap. "There! And I'm sure I hope it'll come in useful."

Dazedly, the old lady looked down at the sheaf of bank notes on her knees and then, with trembling fingers, began to tuck them into her purse. She rose then and lifted wet, faded blue eyes to Grandma's dour angular face. "My, but you're kind, kind," she said earnestly. "How in the world am I ever to thank you?"

"Ach, wheest, woman!" said Grandma with the testiness of embarrassment. "The Lord's the one for you to thank. It was all His doin'."

But Mrs. Macleod was too grateful to be put off so easily, and spots of colour were flying on Grandma's cheeks before she closed the door on her and came back to the sitting room.

"Well?" she demanded of my parents. "Are you satisfied now? Didn't I do what I said I would?"

"Not quite," my father said. "You've profited Mrs. Macleod, confounded a rogue and shamed nobody. But I don't see where your own profit comes in."

"Then you must be blind, Robert," said Grandma. "If the tappit hen's worth twenty-five guineas today it'll be worth more as time goes by. Am I right or wrong?"

My father nodded, a smile creeping into his eyes. "You're right, of course. I hadn't thought of it that way. A slow yield but a sound investment."

"Aye," said Grandma, "and that's only part of my profit. The lesser part."

My father's eyebrows lifted. "Oh? How else do you profit?"

"I wonder that you need ask." Light came into Grandma's grey eyes and the grim old face softened. "How else than in havin' served the purposes of the Lord?"

GRANDMA

. . . and the Booming Bass

REPLETE WITH vanilla ice cream, a tin of toffee in my
pocket and a stick of peppermint rock in my hand, I followed
Grandma from the business section of Ardrach along the shore
road toward home. That morning, a Monday early in July, we
had arrived together from my home in Angusburg, where
Grandma had spent the month of June; and though on our way
down there had been nothing in her dour unbending manner
to suggest that she was glad to have me with her for the summer
months, I knew that this evening trip into town and the visits
to the Tally ice cream parlour and the sweetie shop was her
own way of expressing gratification at my presence.

Sucking contentedly at a piece of the rock, I was half-
trotting beside her gaunt dark striding figure, when, just as we
cleared the United Free Kirk, a blast of sound smote my ears—
a fine, and only too familiar, bass voice roaring out tipsily
the words to "Nicæa":

"Holy, holy, holy, Lord God Almighty!
Early in the morning our song shall rise to Thee . . ."

Grandma stopped short and frowned at the squat red-
sandstone cottage nestled behind its square of garden near
the Kirk.

"Mercy on us!" she said. "Is not that a cryin' shame!"

"Why, Grandma?" I said. "This is Monday."

"Aye, laddie, it's Monday, right enough. But this is his first outbreak in more than six months, and it wouldn't have happened if I'd stayed home and kept an eye on him. Ever since the winter, when I got him in the habit of droppin' by regularly for a bit hymn-sing he hasn't taken a drop, and he was even gettin' so's he'd let out a cheep or two in Kirk. But there—I'm back now, and I'll just make it my business to get him into the choir. Aye, and without a dram in him to keep his courage up, either."

"I don't see why he should need a dram," I said. "After goin' without for six months."

"Don't judge him, Duncan!" said Grandma sharply. "Not that I could approve his drunken hymn-singin' under any circumstances. But I know he means no irreverence and, what's most important, so does the Lord."

Which, coming from Grandma, the sworn enemy of drink and the defender of all things sacred, was a surprisingly moderate pronouncement. But, then, all things are relative, and when I remembered the summer before and the sore problem Captain Dougal Menzies had been to Ardrach and, particularly, to the congregation of the United Free Kirk, I could understand her attitude. Besides, it had been Grandma, alone of the entire congregation, who had had the courage to tackle and solve that problem, and it was only natural, therefore, that she should be disposed to leniency. . . .

When, more than a year before, Captain Dougal Menzies, retired, returned to his native village and bought the cottage by the U. F. Kirk, it was as if he were a complete stranger. It was fifty years since he had gone to sea, a boy of seventeen and the only son of Robert Menzies, grocer, and elder in the U. F. Kirk. Now his parents and many of his contemporaries were in their graves, others moved away, and there were only a few who remembered him, none at all who would have recognized him.

At first, Ardrach had been inclined to dislike the Captain. He was a big man, powerfully built and well-preserved, with cold menacing blue eyes and a strong hard mouth in no wise softened by his bristling close-cropped mustache. Actually, he was always civil enough in his dealings with the villagers, but in his deep resonant voice he carried the habit of authority and, obviously, was not one with whom liberties might be taken, and they took him to be overbearing and superior.

But gradually the Captain began to show himself in a better light. Before moving into the cottage he had it completely renovated and, unlike most of the summer visitors, was at pains to see that the work was done by local firms only. Then he joined the U. F. Kirk and, during these first weeks in Ardrach, was among its most faithful adherents, present at every service and every Wednesday-evening Bible class; always very much his own man, it is true, yet somehow at one with them in their devotions.

It was his open-handedness, however, that finally drew them to him. Not only did he contribute generously to the kirk's various funds and causes, but in any other way in which his money might be useful. As for instance, in the matter of the organ: Wondering why no psalm or hymn was ever sung in full, he learned that because of that instrument's wheezy and oft-patched bellows, old Mrs. MacCall, the organist, got cramps in her legs if called upon for more than three or four verses. A week later a new and more expensive organ arrived from Glasgow and was installed at his sole expense.

Which, in a way, was a curious thing for him to have done, the congregation thought. For devout though he was, the Captain was apparently without musical ability. True enough, those near him in kirk were sometimes aware during the singing, of a strange muted rumbling, hardly melodic yet not discordant; but for the most part he would stand there, tight-lipped and silent, while around him the congregation lifted their voices in praise. Poor fella, was their conclusion, he would like to sing but he just didn't have it in him.

Wherein, as they were to discover, they were badly mistaken. . . .

On a Sabbath in June the evening service of the U. F. Kirk had just come to an end. Soft strains were rising from the new organ and the congregation were beginning to move toward the door, when from somewhere outside the kirk a powerful bass voice broke suddenly into song:

"Worship the Lord in the beauty of holiness;
Bow down before Him, His beauty proclaim . . ."

A startled silence fell on the kirk, and even the organ

faltered in a discord. Then as the stentorian, but oddly discomposed, voice finished the verse and went on to a second, a rustle of whispers and muted exclamations passed over the congregation. It had been noted that for once the Captain had been absent from kirk that Sabbath, but no one had even imagined the nature of his indisposition. Shocked now at the thought of his condition and, even more, at his desecration of the Sabbath, they dispersed quickly and, almost shamefully, hurried away to their homes.

All that evening and throughout the next day the vicinity of the kirk reverberated with intermittent bursts of psalmody. Then on the Tuesday the Captain, red-eyed and haggard, emerged from his cottage and, ignoring the curious glances he met on his way, walked firmly into town and back. Neither then nor at any time later did he offer any explanation for his behaviour, and there was no one with temerity enough to ask for one. But as weeks rolled by without a repetition of the incident, Ardrach, not unmindful of benefits received, decided to take the charitable view. It had just been an accident, they told one another, arising, no doubt, from his lonely bachelorhood, and the Captain returned to grace.

Early that July I came down as usual to stay with Grandma, and on the first Sabbath morning of my visit accompanied her to kirk. Elder Thomas Burns was standing by the plate as we came through the doorway. He returned Grandma's terse greeting and then leaned toward her confidentially.

"I'm feared we're in for it, Mistress Guthrie," he whispered dolefully. "The Captain's in his cups again."

Grandma slipped her offering in the plate and then looked up at him, her grim mouth tight. "Singin'?"

"Aye. Late last nicht an' early this mornin'. Jist the least wee thing an' sure as daith, he'll break oot again."

Apparently the knowledge was general, for as we took our places I noticed that an unusual amount of whispering was going on among the congregation. And, later, when we arose for the first hymn, it was obvious that many were holding back, afraid, of course, of arousing the Captain to renewed efforts. But as the singing went on without interruption, they took heart and began to let their voices go in the usual fullhearted way.

68

The singing safely over, the Reverend Mr. Herbert Dunlop rose in the pulpit and in sonorous voice re-read the text. Then, as was his habit, he grasped the sides of the lectern firmly and looked slowly around the auditorium. "Brethren," he said — and at precisely that instant the expectant hush of the building was shattered by a blare of sound:

"Sunset and evening star,
And one clear call for me . . ."

Appropriately enough, considering the singer, it was Tennyson's lovely and moving "Crossing the Bar."

After the first instant of shock, Timmy Ray, the beadle, rose and hastened to close the window ventilators. But, as became at once evident, this was very little help. No paltry contrivance of wood and glass could hope to muffle that plangent brazen-throated voice. Gamely Mr. Dunlop went on with his sermon, but for once he failed to hold the attention of his listeners. The Captain was going all out now, and from then until the end of the service his thundering bass dominated the minds and ears of the congregation.

This time the U. F. Kirk was seriously upset. So much so that in spite of its being the Sabbath, the elders gathered by the door after the service and, with the congregation around them, held an emergency meeting. Something simply had to be done, they agreed. But the question was, what? To invoke the law was out of the question; the disturbance of a church service was a serious offence and the Captain had been too good a friend to the kirk to be subjected to the stiff penalty involved. Their only course, then, they decided at length, was to appoint a committee of three to approach the Captain and try to reason with him.

But here new difficulties arose to confound them. Elder Burns, it seemed, might have to be away all the next week. Elder Mackay was putting on a sale at his draper's shop and lacked the time. Elder Turnbull declared himself willing to serve on the committee, but his heart was bad and the doctor warned him against undue excitement. And so it went, until it became evident that no committee was to be appointed.

Through all this Grandma had been listening intently, her deep-set grey eyes brightening with anger.

"Shame on the lot of you!" she blared suddenly. "Jinkin'

69

around like a lot of frightened weans! Where's your faith? He's only a man like yourselves and the Lord is on your side."

A murmur of approval rose from the meeting, and the elders exchanged abashed and guilty glances.

"That's a' very weel, Mistress Guthrie," Elder Mackay said, his face red. "But how wad you like to try checkin' the Captain?"

"Like it?" said Grandma. "I'd consider it a privilege. Just say the word and I'll be happy to act for you. And for the Lord."

Again a murmur passed over the meeting.

"Then if ye do," said Elder Mackay, "I'll go wi' ye."

"An' me," said Elder Turnbull. "Bad hert or no'."

"You'll do nothin' of the kind," snapped Grandma. "Either of you. Your hearts are not in it and you'd be nothin' but a hindrance to me. If I go, I go alone."

The elders looked at one another, and there was no mistaking the relief on their faces.

"But, Mistress Guthrie," said Elder Turnbull, "dae ye think it's safe? He's no' the kind tae thole interference an' he micht turn on ye."

Grandma's eyes glinted. "That's a game two can play, Mr. Turnbull."

The Elder shook his head wonderingly. "What'll ye say tae him?" he asked with curiosity.

"I haven't a notion. When the time comes the Lord'll tell me."

"But wad it be proper?" put in Elder Burns. "A weedow lady like yersel' an' him withoot even a skivvy in the hoose?"

Grandma's nostrils flared, a sure sign of amusement. "I'll take my grandson, here, with me," she said. "That'll save my reputation. Or the Captain's . . ."

On Wednesday word came that the Captain was again his usual self, and that evening Grandma and I set out for his cottage. In spite of all I had heard of him as a creature of wrath and violence, it never occurred to me to be afraid. I was with Grandma, a tower of strength, and equal, I believed, to any situation no matter how awkward or precarious.

It was just turning dusk as we walked up the pathway to the cottage. Grandma marched up the steps and without

70

hesitation rapped on the door with the handle of her umbrella. A brief wait, then it swung open and a huge man with inflamed blue eyes glared out at us.

"What is it?" he demanded. And then I saw surprise come into his face. "It's you, Mistress Guthrie?"

"Aye, it's me," said Grandma evenly. "I'd like a word with you, Captain Menzies."

The Captain's eyes narrowed. "What aboot?" he said suspiciously, his great bulk still blocking the doorway.

"Mercy!" snapped Grandma. "Am I a beggar that you keep me on your doorstep? Where's your manners, man?"

The Captain's hard face darkened ominously, and they glared at each other, two fearless iron-willed people, each struggling for ascendancy over the other — diamond cut diamond. Then the Captain's eyes shifted and he moved back. "Come in," he said curtly.

I followed Grandma into a small cosy sitting room, full of golden light from the paraffin lamp hanging in gimbals. She motioned me to a chair in a corner and then took one of the armchairs by the fireplace, sitting rigidly upright, her gloved hands clasped on the head of her umbrella.

The Captain closed the door and came over and stood with his back to the mantel, towering over her. "Well?"

"Sit down, man, where I can see you," said Grandma. "I've no mind to get a thraw in my neck."

The Captain hesitated and then scowling, complied.

"That's more like it," said Grandma. "You know why I'm here, I suppose?"

"Aye." The Captain's voice was a growl. "I know. Fine do I know. An' you'd be the one they'd send," he added, with a sort of grudging admiration. "The only one that'd dare come. Jist the same, Mistress Guthrie, my drinkin's no concern o' yours, or theirs."

"You're right enough there," said Grandma. "Your drinkin's the Lord's concern, and I'll leave Him to judge you."

The Captain's scowl deepened in puzzlement. "Then if it's no' my drinkin', what is't?"

"I'm here," said Grandma, "to ask you, as one kirk member to another, if you won't stop interruptin' the services with your untimely singin'."

71

"Sit down, man, where I can see you," said Grandma.
"I've no mind to get a thraw in my neck."

I saw red creep up the Captain's thick neck. "Tae hear ye, a body would think I did it on purpose."

"We'll not talk about why you do it," said Grandma dryly. "The thing is, there's no need of you doin' it and you can put a stop to it."

The Captain's mouth twisted. "Aye," he said bitterly, "it's easy enough to say, but little do ye know. Mistress Guthrie, I can't put a stop to it."

"Can't or won't?"

Anger leapt in the inflamed eyes. "Can't is what I said an' can't is what I meant!"

"Then you have my pity," said Grandma, unmoved. "A body's in sore straits when he can't avoid offendin' the Lord."

"I'm not offendin' the Lord!" thundered the Captain. "It's just simply—" He sat back suddenly in his chair. "I'm no' in the habit o' explainin' mysel'," he growled.

"Aye, I daresay," said Grandma. "But don't pride yourself on it, you poor creature: for it's a sad weakness, as I know to my cost. It eases a body whiles to open his heart to another. A trouble shared is a trouble lightened."

"Maybe so," grunted the Captain. "But I've no fancy tae share my trouble wi' the hale village."

I saw Grandma's eyes flare, but she restrained herself. "If there's one ounce of decency in you," she said icily, "you'll beg my pardon for that."

The Captain glared at her, his blue eyes fighting hers. Then he looked down at the floor. "I beg yer pardon," he muttered. "I know fine ye're no' the one tae betray a confidence."

"And I knew you knew it," said Grandma. "So?"

The Captain was silent for a little, and then threw her a quick, almost furtive, glance. "Ye think I'm jist a drunkard," he said with difficulty. "But ye're wrong. It's jist simply that withoot the drink I can't have the singin'."

Grandma's heavy eyebrows drew together. "If you say so, I believe you," she said. "But I'm still a long way from understandin'."

"Aye," the Captain said. "For it's a long story. It goes back tae sea. Before that I'd aye been a great one tae sing an' was dearly fond o' music. An' o' a' music I liked best the

73

auld hymns. No doubt ye'll think I must o' had a rare conceit o' mysel', but I knew I had the voice, an' my greatest pleasure when I was wee was to stand by the harmonium an' sing hymns while my mother played for me.

"But when I went tae sea it was a different story. Sailors live a hard life an' are a hard lot, an' they had no patience at a' wi' me an' my hymns, an' many's the kick and skelp I got that first year. On the other hand, I couldna abide the vulgar trash they liked, so the upshot was that I never opened my mooth.

"But I suffered, I'm tellin' ye. There I'd be, lyin' in my bunk or doin' my trick at the wheel, an' they'd come crowdin' into my mind, the braw auld tunes — the Auld Hundred, St. Margaret, Laudes Domini, Melita — bubblin' up inside me till I'd near go daft frae the pressure, but no' darin' tae let oot a cheep.

"An' in the end I did go daft, kinda. By the time I was twenty it was as if my throat had closed up an' I couldna sing, no' even in kirk."

"Well, I never!" said Grandma. "You poor creature!"

The captain gave no sign of having heard her. "But I found a way," he went on. "I'd never been a drinkin' man, but one nicht after I got my third mate's ticket I went ashore wi' the second, an' because it was Hogmanay I let him persuade me into takin' a dram. It was an eye-opener tae me. It released somethin' in me, an' a' the way back tae the ship an' after I was in my room, I jist let it pour oot o' me, hymn after hymn after hymn, till I was drained dry an' eased an' healed.

"An' that's been the way o' it ever since. But now it's come tae be a bad thing, too. For once I get the drink in me I don't know when tae stop. But bad thing or no', when the cravin' to lift my voice comes there's only the one thing for me to do." The Captain raised his head and looked at Grandma. "So there ye are, ma'am. Now dae ye see why I can't promise tae stop interruptin' the kirk services?"

"Aye," said Grandma, "I see. And I'm sure you have my sympathy." But I knew she was distressed. She had been so sure that the Lord would guide her toward a solution of the kirk's problem, but now it looked as if the Lord, for once, had failed her. "It's a sorry lookout for the kirk, though," she said soberly.

74

"Aye, ma'am, an' I regret it. But what can I do?"

"I don't know." Grandma gave a sigh, and then sat looking at him, her grey eyes dark and brooding. "The Lord must have felt for ye, though. For in spite of your drinkin', He's allowed you to keep your health and has brought you safely through your spells when you might well have wrecked your ship."

The Captain looked up quickly. "There was never any danger o' that, ma'am. If my ship was at sea when the cravin' took me, I waited till we made port. My owners' interests had to come first."

To my surprise I saw Grandma's face fill with anger. "You great dreigh creature!" she blazed. "Do you know what you're sayin'?"

"Eh?" The Captain's jaw sagged. "What's that, ma'am?"

"Your owners' interests, indeed! What about the Lord's interests?"

The Captain looked at her perplexedly. "I don't follow ye, ma'am."

The anger cleared from Grandma's face. "No, I see you don't," she said with a moderation of tone. "But it's the answer I've been lookin' for. Captain, these spells of yours never last a whole week, do they?"

"Faith, no!" said the Captain. "Two days, never more'n three. What way do ye ask?"

"There!" said Grandma. "Fool that I was to think the Lord would desert me at a time like this! Captain Menzies, the next time you feel a spell comin' on, could you not think of the Lord's interests and hold off till the next Monday? Then when the Sabbath came you'd be all over it."

"My conscience!" The Captain stared at her. "Of course! An' that's jist what I will do. But why in the blazes did I no' think o' it mysel' long ago?"

"For the best of reasons," said Grandma: "Because it was too simple." She rose, grim and unsmiling, yet with a radiance about her. "So there, Captain. The Lord has solved our problem and now I'll away and leave you in peace."

The Captain got to his feet and stood looking down at her. "Mistress Guthrie," he said humbly, "I'm deeply obleeged tae ye. I wish I could tell ye hoo much."

75

"Are you, now?" said Grandma. "Then, Captain, to prove it, just drop by some evenin' for a hymn or two and let me play the harmonium for you."

"Ach, I couldna, I couldna. Ye know that."

"I know nothin' of the kind," said Grandma. "If you could do it when you were wee, you can do it now. All you need is to get used to the idea again."

The Captain shook his head. "It's useless, ma'am. Useless."

Grandma's face hardened. "I told you you had my sympathy," she said sharply, "but I have little sympathy for a body that's offered help and is too much of a weaklin' to take it."

The blood surged into the Captain's face, and I braced myself for an angry outburst. Then the colour faded away and I saw his hard mouth twitch. "My, but ye're a caution, ma'am," he said, admiration in his voice. "There's no' many would dare say a thing like that tae me. An' maybe ye're richt. At any rate, it wouldna hurt tae give it a try."

"Indeed, not," said Grandma. "The Lord has just solved one problem for us, and He can just as easily solve this one." . . .

On a Sabbath morning in July two years after the Captain gave Grandma his promise, I sat with her in kirk, waiting for the service to begin. Since my arrival the day before, I hadn't thought to ask her what progress she was making with the Captain, but as the choir filed in and took their places, I stared and then turned quickly to her.

"The Captain!" I said under my breath. "Then you did it?"

Grandma glanced at the big hard-faced man sitting at the back of the choir. "Aye," she whispered. "With the Lord's help. Not one drop has he had since that evenin' last summer."

But, later, when we rose to sing and I heard the Captain's magnificent voice giving depth and value and beauty to the singing, I knew that what she had accomplished was far more than his reformation.

GRANDMA
... and the Maid Forlorn

WE WERE sitting out on the front lawn that September evening. My parents, who believed in comfort, lolled back at their ease in canvas chairs, but Grandma, who disapproved of what she called "sprawlin' around," had brought a straight chair from the hall and was perched stiffly on its edge, her fingers busy with her knitting.

I was sitting on the grass with my head against my mother's knee, wondering uneasily how long it would be before I was sent into the house to do my lessons, when the familiar voice of Mr. Petrie rose in the quiet air, shrill with rage:

"You'll do as you're told, my lady! Mind you that! I'll have obedience or out on the street you'll go, and without a penny!"

"Gracious!" Grandma directed her grim hawk-like profile at the sandstone "villa" on the other side of the hedge. "Can it be his housekeeper he's roarin' at, the ill-tempered old carle?"

"Oh, I forgot about that," my mother said. "He doesn't have a housekeeper now, Mamma. This ward came to live with him and he let Mrs. Brodie go." She grimaced. "He's nothing if not thrifty."

"Ward?" said Grandma. "What ward?"

"A Jeanie Cameron from Dalry — just a lassie of twenty-

77

two. Her father was a widower, and when he died in the spring they found that he'd named Mr. Petrie as her guardian. There were no relatives, it seems, and Mr. Petrie was his lawyer."

"An ill thing to have done, surely," said Grandma. "Puttin' her at the mercy of a crankous old wretch like him."

"Ill enough," my mother said. "But from what she says I gather her father was even worse than Mr. Petrie, so in spite of his ill-treatment of her, she feels that she's no worse off."

"But what way does she put up with his ill-treatment?"

"What else can she do? The income from her money goes to him till she's thirty or marries."

"And she won't marry," my father added. "Not if old Petrie can help it. Her chances would be better in a convent."

It was then, as if invoked by the mention of his name, that Mr. Petrie's voice rose again, the words indistinguishable this time but the tone an infuriated blare. Then a girl screamed piercingly, her voice falling away in an anguished moan, and again there was silence.

It was by no means the first time I had heard Jeanie Cameron scream but, as ever, a kind of horror seized me and, instinctively, I looked across at Grandma. She was rising from her chair, her grey eyes ablaze, her mouth a thin hard line.

"My faith!" she grated. "Strikin' the poor thing! I'll go over there and I'll give the cowardly old limmer the blowin'-up of his life!"

"No!" My mother shot out of her chair and grasped her arm. "You musn't, Mamma. You mustn't interfere."

Grandma jerked her arm away. "Don't be daft, Jessie Mackinley! Of course I'm goin' to interfere. I'll sort the old blackguard, see if I don't."

"But, Mamma, you don't understand. Anything you do will only make things worse for her. We know . . . Don't we, Robert?"

"She's right," my father said. "The kindest thing is to leave them alone. If you blow him up he'll just take it out on her later."

"But the thing's preposterous," protested Grandma angrily. "What do we have a law for? A charge of assault would make him sing a different tune."

78

"It would," my father said. "But she won't make it. I know, because I've suggested the same thing and she refused to consider any such course."

"What way not?"

My father shrugged, "Dear knows. But if she won't help herself there's nothing anyone else can do. Nothing."

"Havers!" Grandma sat down with obvious reluctance. "When it's the Lord's business you're on there's always somethin' to be done."

And, knowing her, I was quite certain then that something would be done . . .

The next afternoon, taking advantage of Grandma's presence, my mother went up to Glasgow on a shopping trip, and when I came home from school I found the old lady perched on her straight chair on the lawn, still busily knitting.

"Well, laddie?" she said dourly, as I stopped before her. "Have you been a good boy?"

I grinned happily at her dark unsmiling face. I had never heard her laugh, had never known her to kiss me or offer any other overt mark of affection, yet for all her undemonstrativeness I both loved and had confidence in her. "I'm always a good boy," I said.

"Aye." She sniffed expressively. "I'd be feared for you if you were." And I recognized the little jab she gave me with her knitting needle for the masked caress it was.

Across the hedge the Petrie door closed with a bang. A moment later its owner hurried past us, his thin deeply lined face knotted, as always, in a scowl.

Grandma followed him with hard combative eyes and then turned to me.

"Duncan, how well do you know this Jeanie Cameron?"

"Pretty well. She's real nice, Grandma. You'd like her."

"Would I, now?" Grandma dropped her knitting and rose. "Then maybe you better take me over and introduce me."

As we walked down to the gate and up the Petrie walk I was aware of a tingle of excitement. Now, I thought happily, things were beginning to happen. At the door I rang, and after a little it opened a few inches and a single blue eye peered out at us.

"It's only me, Miss Cameron," I said. "I brought my Grandma over to meet you."

The door was motionless, as though the girl were hesitating, and then it swung slowly open, and I saw with shock the badly discoloured eye she had been trying to hide.

"How do you do, Miss Cameron?" said Grandma, her sharp old eyes on the girl's bruised but still appealing sweet-mouthed face. "I'm Mrs. Guthrie, in case you don't know."

"How do you do?" the girl returned faintly. She stood looking at us uncertainly, almost fearfully, and then said, as if against her will, "Won't you come in?"

We went in, and were shown into the sitting room.

"Mercy, lassie!" said Grandma, as we sat down. "That's a nasty lookin' eye you have there."

"Yes." The girl raised a slender hand to her bruised cheek bone. "I bumped it."

"Aye," said Grandma dryly. "You bumped it. Lassie, why on earth do you not go to the police?"

"Oh, no! I—I couldn't. It would be terrible—frightful."

"It would, indeed," said Grandma. "For him—the blackguard. If you'll let me, I'll be more than pleased to act for you."

"No! Oh, no!" The girl's agitation increased. "Please! I couldn't stand it—all the talk there'd be and having to appear in court. Mr. Mackinley wanted me to do the same thing but it would be shameful—a disgrace."

Grandma sat looking at her in silence, her grim old face inscrutable. And then she gave a little sigh. "Aye, you poor wee soul," she said. "What you need is a protector. Someone who has the right. Have you no kin folk at all?"

The girl shook her head. "None."

"You're sure? There's not many in this world lackin' an uncle or a cousin or even a second cousin."

"Well, there was John," the girl said. "My half brother by my father's first wife. But when I was wee he quarrelled with my father and ran away to sea. I don't know where he is now and wouldn't know him if I saw him."

"And there's nobody else?"

"Nobody." Steps sounded outside on the pavement, and the girl leapt to her feet, a hand flying to her breast. "Oh!" Her body sagged in relief. "For a minute I thought it was him."

80

She turned to us, apology on her face. "I'm awful sorry, but would you mind going now? He'll be back soon, and if he found you here . . ."

Grandma rose at once. "Aye, poor lassie," she said with gruff gentleness. "We'll leave you. But I'll be next door for a week or two and I'll not forget you."

"Thank you." Already the girl had the door open. "You're very kind, but I'll be all right."

That evening Grandma was unusually quiet and thoughtful, and I guessed she was pondering ways and means of helping Jeanie Cameron. The next morning after breakfast she disappeared from the house and for three days I saw practically nothing of her.

On the afternoon of the third day I came home from school to find her and my mother sitting out on the lawn. It was unusually warm, even for the beginning of September, and across the hedge I saw that Mr. Petrie and his ward had sought the coolness of the garden.

I said, yes, I had been a good boy, and, yes, I had worked hard at school. Then, sensing that the business which had kept her away for three days was now finished, I said, "But where have you been, Grandma? What were you doin'?"

She looked at me with a little gleam in her eyes. "I've been seekin', laddie. And not in vain."

I grinned. "Seekin' what?"

"Somethin' I'd just about despaired of findin'."

"Really, Mamma," my mother said uneasily, "I wish you'd speak out. What have you been doing?"

"You'll know very soon, Jessie," said Grandma. She turned at the sound of approaching footsteps. "Within minutes, in fact," she added with significance.

I followed her gaze and saw a young man in the natty blue uniform of a ship's officer coming along the pavement. He was tall and muscular with a strong cheerful blue-chinned face and a short pugnacious nose. As he came abreast of us he looked around and, to my astonishment, winked at Grandma, and, with even greater astonishment, I heard her little snort of amusement. "Impudent chiel!" she grunted.

I suppose I should have guessed something of the truth then, but it was with surprise that I saw the sailor open the

*I followed her gaze and saw a young man in the natty blue
uniform of a ship's officer strolling along the pavement.*

Petrie gate and start across the lawn. Grinning, he came to a stop by the lawn chairs.

"Well?" barked Mr. Petrie. "What do you want?"

The sailor ignored him. "Jeanie Cameron," he said, looking down at the girl. "No mistake about that, for you have the look of your mother."

"Yes." The girl rose, wonderment on her face. "Who—who are you?"

"A fine thing!" The sailor chuckled. "Not to know your own brother!"

"Brother! You—you're not John Cameron?"

"Aye, Jeanie, it's me. I heard a while back that Father was dead and wondered what had become of you, but it wasn't till this mornin' I found out where you were."

The girl was looking up at him with wide blue eyes. "John Cameron!" she said. "But you—" She was silent, and then said, "I'm awful glad you found me, John."

"No gladder than I am, Jeanie. I needed you, for you're the only kin I have in the world."

"Just a minute, you." Scowling, Mr. Petrie got to his feet. "You claim to be John Cameron but how do we know who you are? Let's see your proof."

The sailor turned and eyed him coldly. "Who's this, Jeanie?"

"Mr. Petrie, my guardian. Appointed by Father."

"Aye." The sailor's voice hardened. "That would be Father. Does he treat you right, this sour wee man?"

The girl hesitated briefly. "Yes. All right."

"You're sure? I see you've had a dunt on the eye. It wasn't him did it?"

"Look here!" said Mr. Petrie with alarm in his voice. "What do you mean, coming here and—"

The sailor turned. "Shut up," he said quietly, and Mr. Petrie subsided.

"Was it him did it, Jeanie?" the sailor repeated menacingly.

Again the girl hesitated, and I saw Mr. Petrie turn pale. "No, John," she said at last. "I ran into something in the dark."

"I'm glad to hear it," said the sailor. "For it would be an ill thing if I had to clout an old man like him. But, Jeanie." He raised a huge tanned fist. "Ill thing or no, I'll smash him or any other man that ever lays a finger on any sister of mine."

Mr. Petrie's mouth opened, closed, then he turned suddenly and scuttled into the house.

"Thank you, John." The girl's voice was grave but I could see that her eyes were dancing. "I'm quite sure you'll never need to touch him." She motioned to the chair vacated by Mr. Petrie. "But sit down and tell me about yourself."

"I can't, Jeanie," the sailor said regretfully. "We're sailin' in an hour or two and I've got to get back to the ship. But we call at Angusburg three times a week, so you'll be seein' me real often."

A moment or two later the sailor took his leave and, as he passed us, again winked broadly at Grandma.

"Good gracious!" said my mother in affront. "She may be lucky in having found her brother, but she's certainly not to be congratulated on his manners."

I heard the breath whistle through Grandma's nostrils. "My, Jessie, but you're a rare divert. Her brother!"

My mother's eyes rounded. "Well, isn't he?"

"He is not. He's a lad I found down at the harbour, second mate on the *Centaur,* that big cargo boat."

"Good heavens! Mamma, I was sure you said you had found her brother."

"What do you want, lassie?" said Grandma sharply. "Miracles? All I was lookin' for was a sailor who was a gentleman and personable and about thirty-five years of age. And it was a sore trauchle findin' him, I can tell you. But worth it," she added with satisfaction. "He did real well."

"But, Mamma, a total stranger! Surely that's not quite— quite honest."

"Havers!" said Grandma. "Can you build the house without fellin' the tree? All that matters is that the poor lassie'll have a little peace and happiness from now on. . . ."

Which, as it turned out, was an understatement. For the change that came over Jeanie Cameron was almost unbelievable. Three times that first week the pseudo John Cameron called at the house next door, and, like a bud bursting into bloom, the quiet repressed girl blossomed into a happy radiant creature who laughed easily and often and who sang at her work. Even my mother had to admit that Grandma had done well.

Until the middle of the month this happy state of affairs continued, and then, shortly after Grandma left to visit my Uncle Teddy in Glasgow, we became aware that the situation was changing, and for the worse. As he passed us on his way to the Petrie house, we noticed that gradually John Cameron's face was losing its habitual cheerfulness, and as for the girl, it was as if a slow blight had fallen on her. Now she never sang or laughed, but went soberly about her affairs, her blue eyes heavy, her mouth drooping. What, we wondered helplessly, could have happened?

And then Grandma came back.

She was hardly in the house when my mother told her of the developments next door. Grandma heard her out in silence, her deep-set grey eyes narrow and intent.

"Hmmm!" she grunted then. "Now, I wonder?"

But what it was she wondered she kept to herself. . . .

The next morning, a Saturday, I was playing in the front garden when Grandma came out, carrying her knitting and a hall chair. She placed the chair on the pathway near the hedge, perched herself on its edge and busied herself with her knitting. For more than an hour she sat there, rigid and immobile except for her fingers; then the Petrie front door opened and Jeanie Cameron came out on the stoop to shake her duster.

Grandma stood up. "Good mornin', lassie."

"Oh, good morning." The girl hesitated and then came down the steps and over to the hedge. "I didn't know you were back, Mrs. Guthrie. Did you enjoy yourself in Glasgow?"

"Well enough. Though I could do with less stour and stench. But, lassie, it seems to me you're lookin' kind of peely-wally."

The girl lowered her eyes. "I feel all right."

"That cankert old rascal hasn't been ill-usin' you, has he?"

"No, Mrs. Guthrie."

"That's good," said Grandma. "How's your brother keepin'?"

The girl looked up suddenly. "Oh, let's not pretend, Mrs. Guthrie. I know you sent him, and I'm more than grateful, but he's not my brother. I've always known that. The one thing I mind about John is that he was fair like myself, not dark like this John."

Grandma nodded slowly. "Aye, I had a notion you knew." She was silent, her keen old eyes on the girl's face. "If you like," she said deliberately, "I'll tell him to stop comin'."

The girl's eyes opened wide. "No! Don't do that. I—I like him to come." Scarlet suddenly flowed into her face and she wheeled away. "Oh, I must get on," she said in confusion. "Saturday—such a busy day."

Grandma watched her hurry into the house and then turned, her grim old face thoughtful. "So I was right," she muttered. "Now what am I to do?"

To my disappointment Saturday and Sunday passed without further action on Grandma's part and on Monday morning I went off to school. When I came home in the afternoon my mother and Grandma were again out on the lawn, and across the hedge I saw that Jeanie Cameron and the sailor were sitting on the front steps, talking, but with a notable lack of animation.

I had undergone the usual catechism as to my conduct of the day and was squatting on the grass when I heard footsteps pattering along the pavement toward us, and glanced around.

It was Mr. Petrie. He was in a tremendous hurry, his face contorted with anger, his coattails flying behind him like a ship's pennant. He passed us in a rush, tore up the pathway to his house and came to a stop before the couple on the steps.

"You young scoundrel!" he panted. "I knew fine you were up to something!"

The sailor got up, his face darkening. "Have you gone daft?"

"No, I'm not daft, you imposter! I've had a letter about you and you're no more John Cameron than I am. You're a fraud, a criminal!"

The sailor's weathered face reddened. "That does it," he said with despair in his voice. "I'm sorry to have deceived you, Miss Cameron, but he's right. I'm not your brother."

The girl rose, and with surprise I heard her soft laugh. "I know you're not. I always have."

"Wha-a-at!" screeched Mr. Petrie. "You knew! My fine lady, you'll pay dear for that!"

It was a waste of breath. The sailor was staring at the girl's smiling face, his forehead knotted in bewilderment. Then as their eyes clung I saw his gradually clear and fill with light.

"Jeanie," he said huskily, "would you—would you have me?"

"Yes, John!" The girl's voice was radiant. "Whenever you want me."

The angry colour drained from Mr. Petrie's face. "But, Jeanie, you can't mean it, surely?" he whined. "A common sailor like him. You're just throwing yourself away."

The girl turned, open contempt on her face. "A lot you care what he is or what happens to me. All you're concerned about is the income you'll lose when I marry."

The sailor chuckled. "Aye, you made a bad mistake, my wee mannie. You should have let well enough be. But I'm obliged to you. My soul, am I not! I was nearly at my wits' ends with worry." He slipped his arm through the girl's. "And now, if you'll excuse us, we'll take a wee walk. We have a lot to talk about."

Pressed closely together they went down the pathway and along the street, and behind them Mr. Petrie stood watching, his lips working, his face venomous. Then as they disappeared from sight, he swung around and stamped into his house.

"Just like a play!" My mother was starry-eyed. "So romantic! But, Mamma, who do you suppose could have sent that letter?"

"I did," said Grandma.

"You!" My mother's eyes widened in incredulity. "But, good gracious, why?"

"You've just seen why," said Grandma. "I jaloused they were in love but were hamshackled by this Brother John jookery-pookery, each sweirt to speak the truth for the fear of losin' the other. So I concluded I'd best drop Mr. Petrie a line and let him bring the thing to a head."

"Well, I never!" said my mother. "And he certainly did. My, I do hope they'll be happy."

"They'll be happy enough," said Grandma. "But, poor lassie, she's got a shock in store for her."

"Why? What do you mean, Mamma?"

"Do you know his real name?"

"No?" My mother looked at her wonderingly. "What is it?"

Grandma's nostrils flared. "Macgillicuddy," she said. "My faith, what a mouthful—Mrs. Bartholomew Macgillicuddy!"

87

GRANDMA
...and the Flighty Flora

THE TELEGRAM, like so many of its kind, was more notable for compression than intelligibility:

"Meet noon train simply frightful position do not fail. Flora."

"My faith!" Grandma looked at me, a frown on her lean, grim face. "Who, will you tell me, would Flora be?"

A bell was ringing at the back of my head. "It sounds kind of like Uncle Teddy's Flo," I said, referring to the daughter of my physician uncle in Glasgow. "With her, things are aye frightful or ghastly or the like."

"Aye, sure enough," said Grandma. "And this was sent from Glasgow." She snorted. " 'Simply frightful position'— mad creature, she's likely got a sore hangnail."

I grinned. My Cousin Flo, twenty to my thirteen, was noted in the family for her habit of self-dramatization. Apart from that she was pretty, fiery-tempered and as erratic as a water spider, but on the credit side, warm-hearted, generous and deeply affectionate—to me, a fascinating and amusing person to know.

"I wonder why she's comin' to Ardrach?" I said.

"The dear only knows," said Grandma. "She's a bonnie lass and a good lass but I'd just as soon have dealin's with a lunatic."

88

"Will you meet her?" I said.

"I wouldn't be bothered," said Grandma, "but as it happens I have to go in to the butcher's, so I suppose we can stop at the station on the way back."

The butcher's shop in Ardrach was located in the town's narrow cobbled main street. Grandma selected a blood pudding from the row hanging behind the counter and, after a careful examination of the tripe to see that it had been thoroughly cleaned, bought a pound. This much done we left and went along the street to the sweetie shop. There Grandma bought me a poke of what she referred to disparagingly as "snashters" and, having exhorted me not to "fill my belly" with them, led the way to the station.

I was sitting beside her in the waiting room, crunching contentedly at a cinnamon ball, when the noon train came roaring in.

Grandma got up. "Away you and meet her, Duncan," she said. "The feckless thing'll likely have enough luggage for six."

I left the waiting room and wormed my way along the suddenly busy platform. At the far end of the train I found Cousin Flo standing by a first-class carriage with two large portmanteaux at her feet, her large deep-blue eyes searching the crowd. I went up and stopped before her.

"Hello, Flo," I said, a little shyly.

The eyes came around to me in surprise. Then white teeth flashed in a smile of pleasure.

"Dunc!" She seized me in her arms and kissed me. "You horrible old scoundrel! What are you doing here?"

Blushing, I released myself. "School closed because of an outbreak of enteric and Mother sent me down here. Why did you come, Flo?"

"Oh!" The blue eyes widened stricken. "I'd almost forgotten, Dunc, where's Grandma?"

"Back there at the waitin' room."

"Thank heaven! Oh, I'm in such a ghastly mess, Dunc. Positively shattering. But, come on—this is no place to discuss it."

I picked up the portmanteaux and staggered after her as she went tearing off along the platform. Grandma was standing by the waiting-room door, erect, black-clad and austere. I saw her stiffen with disapproval at Flo's undignified approach.

"Oh, Grandma!" Unconscious, apparently, of Grandma's censorious stare, Flo flung her arms around the old lady's neck and clung to her. "I'm so glad to see you," she emoted. "With you I'll be safe."

Grandma thrust her away and glared at her with ruffled indignation. "Daft fliskmahoy!" she snapped. "What are you goin' on about? A body would think Old Hornie was after you."

"Old Hornie!" Flo gave a short tragic laugh. "If only it were!"

"What! Explain yourself, girl."

"Not here, Grandma." Flo threw an apprehensive glance over her shoulder. "We'll get a cab and I'll tell you on the way home."

"A cab?" Grandma was scandalized. "Lassie, what do you think the Lord gave us legs for?"

"But there's my luggage—it's so heavy. Besides, I'd feel safer."

"Mercy! Safer from what?"

"From—from danger. I may have been followed."

The train had pulled out and Grandma looked eloquently around the now deserted station. "Aye, it's easy to see that," she said with irony. "Then have a cab, if you must, but be prepared to pay for it."

"Of course, Grandma. But come on! Please!"

The ancient station cabby relieved me of the portmanteaux and we took places in his equally ancient vehicle.

"Now, my lady," said Grandma, as we cluttered off down the street, "maybe you'll be good enough to tell me what all this mad tiravee's about?"

"It's a man!" Flo's voice was a thrilling whisper. "A perfect horror of a man."

Grandma sniffed: "Aye, I'm sure. Who is he?"

"A man I met in Glasgow. His name's Thomas Hogarth. I—I thought he was honourable and good and we became engaged. Then, suddenly, I found out what he really is—a heartless, unprincipled philanderer—a ruthless beast parading as a man. Naturally, I sent him back his ring and told him never to come near me again, but for a week now he's been following me around, trying to make up to me, until I'm nearly out of my mind."

90

Flo flung her arms around the old lady's neck and clung to her. "I'm so glad to see you. With you I'll be safe."

"Nearly," murmured Grandma. "Did you not go to your parents?"

"My parents!" Flo rolled her eyes. "Father and his old practice! Mother and her clubs and societies! A lot they care about me!"

"Aye, it's a shame. Did you go to them or did you not?"

"Of course. And that's the ghastly thing about it. They just laughed at me. So I told them I was coming down here for refuge, and Father said that was a fine idea, he got all the dramatics he needed in his business. You see?"

"I'm beginnin' to," said Grandma dryly. "So you think this Hogarth'll follow you?"

"Think! I know he will."

"How?" demanded Grandma. "Did you tell him where you were goin'?"

"Certainly not." Flo lowered her eyes. "But he—he's cunning and resourceful and he'll find out."

"Hmm!" Grandma eyed her with cold scepticism as the cab drew up before her cottage. "A braw story, my lady, but it's all in my eye. Now, get out your purse and pay the cabman." . . .

But whatever lay behind Flo's dramatics, it soon became evident that she really did expect Mr. Hogarth to follow her. Lunch over, she took up a strategic position in the sitting room from which she could watch the roadway without being seen, and all afternoon she sat there, a book on her knees but her eyes on the window. Strangely enough, however, as the afternoon wore on without any sign of Mr. Hogarth it seemed as though, instead of being relieved, she became more wistful and sad of eye.

Finally Grandma, whose eagle eye missed little, lowered her knitting. "My gracious, lassie!" she observed. "What are you grievin' about? A body would think you were feared he wasn't comin'."

Flo threw her a quick startled glance. "It's the—the suspense," she stammered. "I can't bear it."

"Aye, the suspense," said Grandma. "For once I'm inclined to believe you. But don't give up hope."

Colouring, Flo looked down at her book and again there was silence in the room. Then, only a moment later, I heard her give a little gasp, and looked up. She was staring at the

92

window and I followed her gaze. Out by the gate a tall slender young man was standing, looking in at the house. He was wearing a tweed topcoat, turned up at the collar against the spring breeze, and a black bowler. He had friendly dark eyes in a rather thin face and a pleasant though firm mouth.

Flo had jumped to her feet. "It's him!" she gasped. "It's him! He did follow me."

Grandma leaned forward and peered out at the stranger. "Well, I never!" She turned to Flo. "So that's your ruthless beast—that poor thrawn peely-wally lookin' object?"

Flo's eyes flashed. "He's nothing of the kind! He's—" She broke off in obvious confusion.

"Go on," said Grandma acidly. "You were sayin'?"

"I—I mean, you can't judge by appearances. He may look harmless but I know him for what he is."

"You tell me so?" Grandma put down her knitting and rose. "Well, we'll just have him in and see what he's up to."

"No!" Flo rushed after her as she marched out to the hall and grasped her by the arm. "No, Grandma! He—he's dangerous."

"Havers!" Grandma shook her arm free. "If he's dangerous, a mouse is a ravenin' beast of prey."

Flo wheeled away and scuttled up the stairway.

"I won't see him," she cried from the landing. "I'll lock myself in my room."

"Suit yourself," said Grandma. "I am goin' to get to the bottom of this." She opened the door and went out on the stoop. "Come here, young man," she commanded.

Mr. Hogarth came slowly up the path and stopped at the foot of the steps, looking up uneasily at the ominous black figure towering above him.

"Well?" demanded Grandma. "What is't you're after?"

"I'm looking," Mr. Hogarth said timidly, "for Miss Flora Guthrie."

"Indeed? And what gars you think Miss Guthrie is here?"

"Her father told me. You're Mrs. Guthrie, her grandmother, are you not?"

I heard Grandma's breath catch. "Aye, I'm her grandmother," she said slowly. "You and my son seem to be real chief with each other?"

Mr. Hogarth smiled diffidently. "Well, in a way. He's known me all my life. We live just across the street from them."

93

"My conscience!" said Grandma. "But I might have known it—the daft camsteary creature. Laddie, what is't you want with her?"

"Then she didn't tell you?"

"Tell me! My faith, did she not! Now I'll hear your side of it."

"Well, it was something I couldn't help," Mr. Hogarth said plaintively. "You see, I told Flo I would have to work that night—I'm articled to a Glasgow lawyer—but during the morning he called me into his office and said he had changed his mind. A niece of his from the north had arrived on a visit, but he and his wife had a dinner engagement and he wondered if, instead of working, I would take the niece to a theatre. At his expense, of course. Well, I couldn't refuse, but I thought it would be as well if I didn't let on to Flo. And that's just where I made my mistake, for Flo and her mother were at the same theatre and saw us."

"Aye, just that," said Grandma. " 'Be sure your sin will find you out.' But what way did you not explain to her?"

"Because she wouldn't let me. She won't listen to a word I say and two letters I wrote her came back unopened."

"Aye, that would be her," said Grandma. "Well, laddie, I'd be glad to help you, but she's locked herself in her room and I doubt she'll stay there. However, come away in and I'll see what I can do."

"No, thank you, Mrs. Guthrie," Mr. Hogarth said hopelessly. "It wouldn't be a bit of good. But if you'd give her a message I'd be much obliged to you."

"Just as you think. What's the message?"

Mr. Hogarth's pleasant mouth hardened. "This thing has gone on long enough, so will you tell her, please, that I intend to stay right in front of this house till she comes out and lets me explain?"

Grandma's eyes glinted. "I will, indeed," she said grimly. "But you'll have a long wait, I'm thinkin'."

"I don't care. Sooner or later she'll have to come out, and then we'll get this thing settled, one way or other."

"Well, I wish you luck, laddie," said Grandma and turned away. "I'll be back and let you know what she says."

She went up the stairway to Flo's bedroom and tapped. "Flora! Open this door."

"He isn't there with you?" Flo's voice came suspiciously.

"No, he is not. Open up!"

The door opened and Flo looked out cautiously. "What did he say?"

"Aye, you deceitful creature!" spat Grandma. "Ruthless beast, indeed—a laddie you've known all your life! You should think shame."

Flo lowered her eyes. "Has—has he gone?"

"No, he has not. And, what's more, he bids me tell you he's stayin' right where he is till you go out and speak to him."

"The cheek of him!" said Flo indignantly. "He must be insane."

"He's nothing of the kind. But, poor fella, he's fair distracted. It was his employer made him take that lassie—a niece of his—to the theatre. And now you'll not give him a chance to explain."

Flo's eyes distended. "His employer's . . . niece!" Then her mouth hardened obstinately. "That's no excuse. He should have told me."

"Aye, so he should. But we all make mistakes, and he thought he was doin' it for the best. Now away out and speak to the lad and have done with this nonsense. It's as plain as the nose on your face that you're in love with him."

"In love with him!" Flo gave a short crackling laugh. "Him! I hate him. Detest him."

"Oh, my conscience!" Grandma's eyes blazed. "You dreich obstinate fliskmahoy, if you're not enough to scunner a body!"

She swung away and marched down the stairs to the front door. Mr. Hogarth was still waiting by the steps.

"Just as I jaloused," said Grandma bitterly. "It's useless. If you're a wise laddie you'll away back to Glasgow and leave her to stew in her own juice. That'll soon bring her to her senses."

"No." Mr. Hogarth shook his head with quiet determination. "Until I know for sure just where I stand with her I can't settle down to work or anything else. I'm staying, Mrs. Guthrie."

"Then come inside, laddie. It vexes me to see you waitin' out there like a homeless messin."

95

"No, thank you, Mrs. Guthrie. It's fine weather and there's no need of me upsetting your household. I'll be fine where I am."

"Well, have it your own way," said Grandma reluctantly. "And, who knows, maybe it's all for the best." . . .

For the rest of that evening until darkness at length hid him from our sight, Mr. Hogarth maintained his lonely vigil. Then the moon came up and from then until bedtime we were able to see his head and shoulders silhouetted against the sky over Arran.

When I came down in the morning I found Grandma standing by the sitting-room window. "Just look at that," she said grimly.

I went over to her side. Mr. Hogarth was sitting on the gravel with his back against a gatepost, his knees drawn up, his head sunk on his chest.

"Crikey!" I said. "He's sleepin'."

A gasp came from behind me, and I turned. Flo had come in and was staring past me, her blue eyes wide.

"Good gracious!" she said faintly. "Has he been there all night?"

Grandma swung on her. "Aye, has he," she snapped. "More's the shame on you."

Flo stiffened. "Why blame me, Grandma? I didn't ask him to stay."

"Faugh!" Grandma gave her a glare of disgust. "I'm a fool to waste my breath on you. Duncan, bring in the milk can and we'll have breakfast."

I had delivered a tray of hot food to Mr. Hogarth—which he accepted with alacrity—and was back at the breakfast table when the door bell rang. Grandma went out and came back presently with an opened telegram in her hand. Her face, I saw with wonderment, was black with anger.

"Just you listen to this, my lady," she said. "It's to me from your father." She raised the telegram. " 'Tom Hogarth's employer threatening discharge imperative return at once love Ted.' Now, Flora Guthrie, what are you goin' to do?"

Flo dissembled the quick alarm I had seen flash across her face. "Nothing," she said coldly. "He's the one you should read that to, not me."

Her fingers trembling, Grandma returned the telegram

96

to its envelope and laid it on the table. "Flora," she said with deadly calm, "you're young and in love and because of that I've put up with your nonsense. But when you go the length of losin' your lad his job and maybe spoilin' both your futures it's high time I took a hand. So pack your bags, my lady, and be ready to leave on the first train for Glasgow."

"Why, Grandma!" Flo's voice was heavy with shock and protest. "You can't mean it—that you'd turn me out and leave me at the mercy of that—that—"

"Ruthless philanderin' beast," snapped Grandma. "Aye, that's just what I do mean."

"I won't go," said Flo rebelliously. "I refuse to go."

Spots of colour gathered on Grandma's cheeks. "You'll go—make no mistake about that. Aye, and before you go you'll make up with your lad so he can go back to his work with an easy mind. That's a promise, girl."

"Never!" Tears came to Flo's eyes. "And I won't go! You can't make me. I'll stay, no matter—" Her voice choked and she jumped up from the table and rushed from the room.

Shocked at her temerity, I looked up at Grandma. She was shaking her head, brooding eyes on the empty doorway.

"Demented," she muttered. "The poor daft lovesick creature—just demented. I should have interfered long ago."

"But what'll you do, Grandma?" I said. "How will you make her be friends with Mr. Hogarth?"

She looked down at me, and behind the grim mask of her face I could sense amusement.

"Does it seem such a hard thing, laddie?"

"It seems impossible," I said.

Her nostrils flared. "And yet it's easy, Duncan. So easy that it's laughable."

And with that I had to be satisfied. . . .

About eleven o'clock Grandma made a trip into town and when she got back, an hour later, we sat down to lunch. It was an uncomfortable meal, Grandma grim and withdrawn, Flo tight-lipped and silent. When it was over and the dishes done, Grandma joined me in the sitting room, and a few moments later Flo came in and took a chair near the door, ready, I guessed, to fly to her room at the first alarm. Outside, Mr. Hogarth stood leaning wearily against a gatepost.

97

We had been there only a few minutes when Grandma got up and opened the window.

"Stuffy," she said, as she returned to her chair. "A breath of fresh air'll do us good."

A half-hour passed, silently except for the click of Grandma's knitting needles. Then several houses away I saw the stalwart, if well-larded, form of Constable Hughie MacCrae come stalking majestically along on his afternoon patrol of the Shore Road. He came steadily on until he was abreast of the slender figure by the gatepost and then stopped, frowning darkly.

"Noo, what's this?" His heavy voice came clearly through the window. "For twenty-four hours ye've been skulkin' aboot here. What are ye up to, my man?"

From the corner of my eye I saw Flo come over to the window.

Mr. Hogarth had straightened. "Don't be silly, Constable. Is there any reason why I can't stand here if I want to?"

"Aye, is there. Loiterin', they ca' it. Forbye, ye look tae me like a gey suspicious character." Which was true enough, for weary, haggard and unshaven, Mr. Hogarth had taken on a faintly disreputable appearance. "I think," said the Constable judiciously, "ye better come alang an' see the Sergeant."

"I'll do nothing of the kind." Mr. Hogarth's voice was high with alarm. "You're exceeding your duty, Constable."

"That'll do," said the Constable sternly, and dropped a massive hand on Mr. Hogarth's shoulder. "Are ye comin' quiet?"

Mr. Hogarth's face flamed. "Take your hands off me!" he cried, and thrust the Constable away from him. "I think you must be mad."

"By Jove!" roared the Constable. "Resistin' arrest an' assaultin' a police officer! Ye'll get six months for this, my lad." He whipped out a pair of handcuffs and after a brief struggle snapped one of them on Mr. Hogarth's wrist. "Noo, ye'll come wi' me," he growled, and began to drag his prisoner away.

A sharp exclamation left Flo. She wheeled away from me, and a moment later I saw her flying down the path to the roadway. She raced past the Constable and then turned and confronted him, her blue eyes like blow-torch flames.

"What do you think you're doing, you big idiot?" she said fiercely. "Leave him alone!"

"Hey?" The Constable frowned down at her. "An' wha micht you be, young leddy?"

"I'm Mrs. Guthrie's granddaughter, that's who I am. Take off those handcuffs!"

"Noo, haud on," said the Constable. "Dae ye ken this man, Miss?"

"Certainly, I do. His name's Thomas Hogarth and he's my fiancé. Now, will you take off those things?"

"Bless us! Wha wad have thocht o' such a thing?" The Constable produced a small key and freed Mr. Hogarth's wrist. "Man," he complained, "what way did you no' tell me ye were her fiancy?"

Mr. Hogarth looked at Flo and gulped. It was an awkward question.

"You could have asked, couldn't you?" snapped Flo. Glaring, she put her arm through Mr. Hogarth's. "Come away in, Tommy," she said protectively, "before he arrests you for breathing or something."

And it was then, as they turned toward the house and I saw the Constable grin and wink past them at Grandma, that the truth came to me.

Grandma had turned from the window and was waiting with gleaming eyes when the reunited couple came in. For all his weariness Mr. Hogarth's face was alive and bright, but Flo, I noted, was unable to meet Grandma's steady stare.

"Well, there," said Grandma. "Now, that's more like the thing, and I'm sure you're both a lot happier. But Flora, you'd best look slippy and get your lad tidied up and fed, for the cab'll soon be here."

"Cab? What cab, Grandma?"

"What other cab," said Grandma, "but the one I ordered to take you and your lad to the station."

Flo gave a start and looked at her fixedly. Then her eyes moved to the open window, and I saw a wave of scarlet wash into her face. "Oh!" It was a gasp of mortification. "It was you—"

"Wheest, wheest, lassie," said Grandma with gruff gentleness. "Whatever I did, you acted like the decent loyal woman I know you to be at bottom, and I'm real pleased with you."

A compliment from Grandma was a rare thing indeed, and I saw the chagrin clear from Flo's face. She glanced up at Mr. Hogarth and suddenly at sight of his slack-jawed mystification, threw back her head in a peal of laughter. "Really, Grandma," she gasped, "you—you're positively—positively—"

"Shatterin'," said Grandma. "Now, away you go, lassie."

The cab pulled away and Grandma and I went back to the sitting room. A question was teasing at my mind.

"But, Grandma," I said, "how did you know that Flo would stop the policeman?"

Her nostrils flared. "I'll tell you a secret, laddie—because I was gey like her when I was twenty and that's what I'd have done myself."

GRANDMA
... and the Spoiled Brat

AS THOSE who have followed these chronicles know, my maternal grandmother was anything but an engaging personality —gaunt, angular and inflexibly erect in appearance; dour, sharp-tongued, autocratic and undemonstrative by nature. It must seem strange, therefore, that as a boy I should have been so deeply attached to her. But looking back now from a perspective of age and experience, I can see that there were sound reasons for this attachment, and I know, too, that placed as I was, almost any child would have been drawn to her.

Take, for instance, the case of Robbie Turnbull.

My first knowledge of Robbie Turnbull was of a spoiled little brat of five, with a thin peaked face and a sullen mouth. That summer when I went to Ardrach to spend my holidays with Grandma, he and his young widowed mother had already moved into the Muir house, only two doors from Grandma's cottage; but with interests of my own to keep me occupied, I saw comparatively little of him, and with that little was quite content. But circumstance, as it turned out, was to lead Robbie Turnbull to an active and intimate place in my life.

It began, really, on an afternoon in July. We were out on the front lawn, Grandma knitting in the shade of the old sycamore tree while I squatted at her feet, rigging a new handline. I had heard the screaming, drawing gradually closer, but intent on what I was doing I paid no attention until I heard Grandma speak.

"My faith." She had lowered her knitting and was frowning along the long slow curve of the Shore Road. "There's no need of that. None whatever."

I followed her gaze. A hundred yards away, Mrs. Turnbull was approaching us slowly, her slender figure bowed forward in the effort of dragging her struggling, vociferating son behind her. Twice while we watched he lay down on the flagged pavement, kicking with rage, and had to be lifted bodily to his feet before she could resume her way.

When, finally, they came abreast of us, Grandma got up and went over to the edge of the lawn.

"What's up with him?" she said abruptly.

Mrs. Turnbull paused and lifted a face full of distress and flushed with warmth and embarrassment. She was a little thing, still in her twenties, with gentle blue eyes and a sweet soft-lipped mouth.

"Is he not awful?" she said. "He wants an ice cream wafer; but he's already had three and I'm frightened to let him have it. Really, Mrs. Guthrie, I don't know what to do with him sometimes."

"Aye, I can see that," said Grandma. "And, what's more important, he doesn't know what to do with you."

"With me?" the girl said in surprise. "I don't understand."

"It's simple," said Grandma. "What that bairn needs is a firm hand. Without it he's like a ship without a rudder, driven helplessly about by the winds and tides of his own fancy, a derelict."

"But what can I do?" the girl said plaintively. "He's only a baby, really, and I can't leather him."

"I don't know why not," said Grandma. "If that's what he needs. But it's not a question of leatherin' him; it's a question of teachin' him that for every misdeed there is surely and certainly a penalty, no matter how slight the penalty may be. For it's not punishment that keeps a bairn from ill-doin', but the certainty of punishment."

"But that seems so harsh," the girl objected. "So—so severe."

"Fiddle-di-dee!" said Grandma. "An undisciplined bairn is aye an unhappy bairn, just like that one of yours. By not bein' firm with him you're doin' him the greatest unkindness in your power."

The girl shook her head. "I couldn't. I couldn't treat him that way. He'd grow up to hate me—" She staggered back a few steps as Robbie yanked suddenly at her hand, and then recovered her balance. "Please, darling! You might have hurt Mother."

Robbie, who had stopped crying, was staring invidiously at Grandma, his lower lip out-thrust. "I hate her," he said. "She's an old beast and I want to go home."

"Robbie!" his mother said. "What a terrible thing to say!" She turned apologetically to Grandma. "I'm sorry, Mrs. Guthrie."

"Don't be sorry for me," said Grandma. "It's not me he hates, the poor wee smout. It's himself."

The girl looked at her in puzzlement, and then, yielding to the tugging of her son's hand, began to move away. "I better get him home while he's in the mood," she said. "Good-day, Mrs. Guthrie."

Grandma stood watching as they resumed their way. "Tragic," she said, shaking her head. "Just tragic. She's a good wee body, kind and gentle, and she loves her laddie dearly. But she'll ruin him. As sure as death, her weakness'll be his undoin'. Her weakness and her selfishness."

"Her selfishness?" I said.

"Aye, just that, laddie. She thinks that by bein' easy with him she's bein' good to him, but the truth is that it's herself she's bein' good to, not him."

It was a day or two after this, just as we were finishing tea, that the doorbell rang. Grandma nodded to me, and I went out to the hall and opened the door. It was Mrs. Turnbull, wide-eyed and pale in the grip of some inner distress.

"Your grandmother?" she said. "Is she in?"

I said, yes, and ushered her into the sitting room.

"Good-day, lassie." Grandma waved to a chair. "Sit you down."

"Oh, now! I can't stay, Mrs. Guthrie. Robbie's asleep, but he might waken any minute."

"That wouldn't hurt him," said Grandma. "Sit down and tell me what's troublin' you."

The girl sank reluctantly onto a chair. "I've just had a telegram. From my father. My mother's critically ill and he wants me to come home at once."

"Well, that's bad news, I'm sure. When are you leavin'?"

"I . . . don't know. It's Robbie, you see. I can't take him with me, Mrs. Guthrie. He's so wild and noisy and my father's not too strong. Yet I've simply got to go."

Grandma's eyes sharpened. "So?"

The girl hesitated. "I—I hope you won't think it presumptuous of me, and if you'd rather not I hope you'll say so, but I was wondering if you'd take care of him for me? I have no one else to turn to."

Grandma was frowning. "I could do that, I suppose."

"Oh, would you! I'd be glad to pay you, of course."

Grandma shook her head. "There'd be no question of pay, lassie. But there would be a question of discipline. He'd have to obey me."

The girl looked at her wistfully. "But you wouldn't be hard on him? He's sensitive, you know, and not very strong."

"I know what he is," said Grandma. "And why." She nodded at me. "Would you say this callant was hard used?"

Mrs. Turnbull looked around at me. I grinned at her and her lips lifted slightly. "No, I wouldn't. He looks very happy. And very healthy."

"And so he is," said Grandma. "Because he's had exactly the kind of treatment I propose to give your laddie. What time do you want to go?"

"This evening, I thought. There's a train for Glasgow at 6.35."

Grandma glanced at the clock. "Then you better get the bairn's things packed and I'll have Duncan here bring them over. And you needn't fash yourself, lassie. I'll not hurt the wee mite."

I won't dwell on the painful scene that took place when Robbie Turnbull learned that he was to stay with Grandma while his mother was away. But long after the cab had driven away, he lay on the sitting-room carpet, his small frame racked by tearing sobs, inconsolable and completely unapproachable. Near him Grandma sat stiffly erect on the edge of a chair, knitting, her face grim, but from time to time I could see her eyes go to him and I knew that inwardly she was distressed.

As they came to the bottom of the stairway he grabbed the newel post and hung on.

Finally, I went over to her. "Maybe if you gave him a sweetie, Grandma," I suggested.

She shook her head. "Get your blocks, laddie, and play with them. But don't speak to him."

I got my box of miniature building blocks and, kneeling on the floor, began the construction of a house. I had laid the first two courses of blocks and was framing a window opening when I noticed that Robbie's sobbing had eased and saw from the corner of my eye that he was sitting up, watching me. I went on with my building and a few moments later he came over and stood beside me.

"I want to play with them," he said sulkily.

I looked at Grandma, and she gave me a little nod. "Here." I emptied about half the blocks on the floor. "You build a house of your own."

"No!" He stamped his foot. "I want them all."

"Half of them," I said. "If you don't want them, Robbie, I'll take them back."

His mouth tightened angrily, and I guessed what he was going to do. When he kicked at my building I blocked his leg with my arm and he sat down on the floor with a thud. Again the room rang with his screams, but following Grandma's example, I paid no attention. After a little they died away and he sat up and began to build his house.

An hour passed peacefully. Then Grandma laid down her knitting and got up.

"Come, Robbie," she said. "Time for bed."

"No!" He thrust his lip out at her. "I'm not goin' to bed."

Grandma took his arm and drew him gently but firmly to his feet. Robbie's face turned crimson and a screech of rage left him.

"I hate you! You old witch, I hate you!"

Her face expressionless, Grandma led him, struggling and crying, out to the hallway. As they came to the bottom of the stairway he grabbed the newel post and hung on.

Grandma released him at once. "All right, my wee mannie," she said. "When you're ready for bed let me know."

She came back to the sitting room and closed the door, and outside, Robbie's screaming rose to new heights.

"My!" Grandma shook her head. "I'll not be sorry when this first lesson's over."

"What lesson?" I said.

"The lesson that all this greetin' and yowlin' are of no service to him whatsoever."

A moment later Robbie's roars began to taper off.

"Maybe he's learnin' it now," I said.

"I wouldn't wonder," said Grandma. "At his age they learn quick."

The crying stopped and for ten minutes there was no sound from the hall. I looked at Grandma. "I wonder what he's doin'?" I said.

106

"Aye, I wonder. Take a keek out the door, Duncan."

I opened the door and peeped out. Robbie was sitting on the bottom step, his face sullen and obstinate.

"Are you ready for bed, Robbie?" I said.

He threw me a look like a blow. "No!"

I closed the door. "Maybe you'll have to punish him," I said.

"No need of that," said Grandma. "He's punishin' himself now as hard as he can. From now on we'll just leave him alone."

I was reading an hour or so later when the clock struck ten.

"All right, Duncan," said Grandma. "Off to bed with you. And mind you say nothin' to Robbie on your way up."

Out in the hallway Robbie was sitting where I had left him. As I came toward him he glowered up at me from under his brows. I went past him without speaking and ran up to my room. Ten minutes later I was in bed and asleep. . . .

I don't know what roused me, for I was anything but a light sleeper, but suddenly I was wide awake, alert. The room was full of moonlight, and over by the door I saw a small forlorn figure. I swung my legs out of the bed.

"Robbie," I said, "come here."

For a moment there was no response, then he came toward me slowly, stumbling, and I realized that he was dead for sleep.

He made no complaint as I began to strip off his clothes. When I had him down to his chemise I rolled him over to the back of the bed and covered him. He gave one little sigh and fell asleep.

I was settling back when Grandma came through the doorway, wrapped in a dressing gown. She went over and peered down at Robbie and then straightened.

"Well, thank goodness," she said. "For two solid hours I've been in my room waitin' to see what he would do. Would you like me to take him to his own room?"

"No, he'll be fine here, Grandma," I said. He had allowed me to undress him and put him to bed and suddenly I was aware of a new tenderness for him. "What way could he not sleep with me always?"

"He can if you like," said Grandma. "Indeed, it would

107

be good for him. One bairn learns from another. Good-night, laddie." She went over to the door and then turned. "You're bein' a help to me, Duncan," she said abruptly. "For he's a handful, the wee thing, and I'm not as young as I was. Good-night."

And as I snuggled down beside Robbie I was glowing. Compliments from Grandma were like gems — rare and accordingly precious. . . .

The next morning began well enough. Intrigued, I think, by the novelty of his new situation, Robbie allowed me to help him wash and dress, but when he sat down to breakfast I saw his lip come out again.

"I don't like porridge," he muttered.

"I daresay," said Grandma. "But it likes you, so eat it up."

Robbie made no move to pick up his spoon. "I want a piece of shortbread. Mamma always gives me a piece of shortbread."

"Aye, I wouldn't wonder," said Grandma. "But I'm not your mamma. Eat up your porridge, though, and you'll get an egg."

"I want an egg now. I'm hungry."

"If you're not hungry for porridge you're not hungry for an egg."

Robbie's mouth began to quiver, but to my relief he made no sound. Apparently he had learned his first lesson. But all through breakfast he sat staring mutinously at the table, and finally Grandma got up and began to clear away.

Robbie watched her, round-eyed. "I want my porridge. I'm hungry."

"That's a pity," said Grandma. "For breakfast's over. But just think what a braw appetite you'll have for dinner."

Robbie's face turned crimson and he stared at her with incredulity. Then as she went on calmly clearing the table, he leapt suddenly from his chair and ran from the house. Watching defiantly over his shoulder, he crossed the road to the beach, and then, finding himself unpursued, sat down on the shingle, his face in his hands.

"Will I bring him back, Grandma?" I said.

"My faith, no! That's what his mother would do, the

poor feckless wee boy. Aye fussin' with him. Far better to leave him there to think things over." She clicked her tongue. "But, ach, it grieves me to have to treat a bairn like this. Thank goodness another twenty-four hours'll see us through the worst of it." . . .

Grandma had to go into town that morning, and I was left at home to keep an eye on Robbie. He was no trouble. A lonely and pitiful little figure, he sat on the shingle, playing sombrely with the stones or staring broodingly at the sea. But when dinnertime came and Grandma called us, he got up at once and followed me to the house.

That was probably the first real meal Robbie had ever eaten. He had soup, a lamb chop with vegetables, custard and two glasses of milk, and packed the lot away with gusto and dispatch. Even then he would have eaten more, but Grandma shook her head, and I noticed that he made no protest.

The tide was on the flood that afternoon and now, dinner over, I got out my handline and got ready to go down to the old stone jetty and try for a flounder. Robbie watched me with solemn grey eyes.

"I want to fish, too," he said to Grandma, but in a tone that anticipated refusal.

"Aye, I had a notion you would." Grandma went to the kitchen press and came back with a paper bag. "Here," she said gruffly, and handed it to him.

Robbie opened the bag and drew out a new handline, complete with frame, sinker and hook. For a little he stared at it and then lifted round wondering eyes to Grandma's dour face. "Is it mine?"

"Aye, it's yours," said Grandma. "But see you don't get that hook in your finger. It'll go in a lot easier than it'll come out."

Light came into Robbie's face and he stood up and looked at me. "Can I go with you, Duncan?"

I nodded, grinning at him, and, for the first time, saw him smile. He turned back to Grandma. "I'll catch you a fish, Grandma," he said with sudden new confidence. "A great big one."

To my surprise I saw tears come to Grandma's eyes.

109

"Ach, away, you wee blether," she snapped, and turned away. "I'll believe in your fish when I see it."

But, strangely enough, he did catch her a big fish — a good-sized flounder — and bore it home in triumph. Grandma received the offering with no more than a grunt of approval, but she lost no time getting it cleaned and that evening, to his vast pride, we had it for tea. . . .

It was from this point on that the new Robbie Turnbull began to emerge. As was only to be expected, he still had a great deal to learn and there were frequent scenes as he pitted his will against Grandma's, but as the days slipped by there was a steady and noticeable improvement in his conduct. At Grandma's suggestion I began to teach him to swim, and now when I went on fishing trips or other expeditions I always took him along. For all of which he rewarded me with a growing affection and companionability.

Now, as the result of exercise and fresh air and a strictly rationed amount of sweets, he always sat down with a good appetite and ate what was placed before him. And when his bedtime came there was never any question about his going. Like me, he knew now that beneath Grandma's crusty exterior there lay a wealth of kindness, but that access to it was possible only through obedience, and profiting, I suppose, from my example, he began to give his obedience cheerfully. By the time three weeks had passed, Robbie Turnbull was well on his way to being a healthy, happy little boy.

In the meantime a steady flow of letters had come from Mrs. Turnbull, reporting her mother's progress but concerned mainly with the welfare of her son. To all of these Grandma replied promptly and reassuringly. And then, late in August, another letter came, saying that her mother was well enough now to be left and that she would be home the next day.

I heard the news with regret, and yet with satisfaction.

"She's goin' to find a big change in Robbie," I said. "Is she not, Grandma?"

"Aye." Grandma shook her head morosely. "But what's the good of it? A week with her and it'll be the old story over again. It seems a hard thing to say, but the truth is that she's the worst enemy the poor wee smout has in the world."

We were in the sitting room after dinner the next day

when the cab stopped outside the Muir house. Watching from the window, I saw Mrs. Turnbull pay the cabman and, leaving her bags at the gate, come hurrying along the pavement. I went out to the hall and had the door open when she came running up the steps. With a smile she went past me into the sitting room. She exchanged quick greetings with Grandma, and then, as she saw Robbie, dropped to her knees.

"Oh, my darling! My darling!" She hugged him and then held him at arms' length. "But how brown you are!" she said, devouring him with glowing eyes. "And I do believe you've put on weight."

"He has that," said Grandma. "Instead of a lot of snashters he's had three good meals every day. Includin' porridge," she added meaningly.

"Porridge?" Mrs. Turnbull looked with surprise at her son. "But, darling, you always said you didn't like porridge?"

Robbie chose to ignore the point. "I can swim," he said.

Mrs. Turnbull laughed. "With one toe on the bottom?"

"No, he can really swim," I said proudly. "He can do the breast-stroke and he's learnin' the trudge."

Robbie chuckled. "And I can dive, too."

"Good gracious!" Wonder-filled eyes on her son, Mrs. Turnbull got up and took a chair. "Why, I can hardly believe it," she said, "the change in him. He looks so healthy and seems so happy. I'm—I'm delighted, Mrs. Guthrie."

"Aye, lassie, you're delighted," said Grandma dryly. "But are you delighted enough to discipline him as I have?"

Mrs. Turnbull's face shadowed. "How can I, Mrs. Guthrie? It was easy enough for you, but I'm his mother and I couldn't bear to have him frightened of me."

"My gracious!" Grandma glowered at her. "You surely don't think he's frightened of me?"

"Isn't he?" Mrs. Turnbull said timidly.

"He is not," said Grandma. "No more than that other laddie there. I keep tellin' you — a disciplined bairn is a happy bairn."

Mrs. Turnbull made no reply, but it was obvious that she was not convinced. She turned to Robbie. "Well, darling, are you ready to go home with Mother?"

Robbie looked at her without replying. And then I saw his mouth begin to tremble. Suddenly, he swung around and

111

ran to Grandma and buried his face in her lap. "I don't want to go home," he wailed. "I want to stay with Grandma."

Mrs. Turnbull stared at him, stupefaction in her face.

"There you are, lassie," said Grandma. "That's how frightened he is of me."

Mrs. Turnbull's eyes filled. "But I don't understand," she said quaveringly. "Why should he prefer you?"

"I've told you why," said Grandma. "Because I disciplined him. Because I gave him the rudder he needed and now he wants to keep it." She took Robbie by the shoulders and straightened him. "That'll be enough greetin', my wee mannie. It's not to China you're goin' but just a door or two away. Will you come and see me tomorrow?"

Robbie blinked and managed a watery smile. "Yes, Grandma."

"That's fine." Grandma gave him a little gentle shove. "Now away you go with your mother."

Obediently, Robbie went over to his mother and, hand-in-hand, they left the house. Standing in the doorway, Grandma and I watched them go down the walk. As they turned onto the pavement Robbie stopped suddenly.

"I want to show you how I can swim, Mamma."

"Yes, darling. But later. I have so much to do."

Robbie's lip came out. "I want to show you now."

"No, Robbie. Now, come along like a good boy."

"No!" Robbie's face turned crimson and he grabbed at a paling and held on. "I want to show you now!" he yelled.

"Will you look at that," muttered Grandma, "just one minute and it starts again. The poor weak wee creature, she'll never learn."

But for once she was wrong.

Red with embarrassment Mrs. Turnbull looked across at us. Her eyes met Grandma's, and suddenly I saw her mouth draw tight. She snatched Robbie away from his paling, drew him against her legs, and with her free hand paddled the seat of his pants, hard.

"There!" She released him, her eyes blazing. "Now will you come home?"

Robbie was screaming with rage and pain. "I hate you! I hate you! You're a beast!"

Instantly Mrs. Turnbull seized him again and repeated the operation.

"Now." She held out her hand. "Come!"

Robbie's screaming had stopped as suddenly as it had begun. For a moment he stood staring up at her with wet astonished eyes. Then he put his hand in hers and together they walked along the pavement.

"Well, there!" said Grandma with satisfaction. "I'll not say it's the method I'd have used myself, but it's a hopeful sign just the same. It looks now as if I've done better than I hoped for."

And, as it transpired, this time she was right.

GRANDMA
... and the Prideful Woman

I HAD just turned twelve when Mrs. Bronach-Kerr descended on Angusburg and, with her teen-aged daughter Jeanie, moved into the old Harvey place at the corner of Kilburnie and Ailsa Roads. She was a widow and obviously, even ostentatiously, well-to-do; a large angular woman with cold blue eyes and a distant supercilious manner and, as she lost no time in impressing on the community, a vastly superior person. Her father had been none other than that self-made knight of industry, Bronach the soup man (Bronach's Desiccated Soups — A Meal in a Mouthful), while her husband had been one of the Kerrs of Strathdoon, a well-known if not well-off branch of that family. All of which, it seems, required her to be extremely discriminating in her choice of acquaintances, and it was her habit, therefore, to cut and snub ruthlessly all those she deemed beneath her in social or economic position.

But as the Book warns us, "Pride goeth before destruction, and an haughty spirit before a fall," and one day Mrs. Bronach-Kerr was to reap where she had so carefully sown. . . .

To be exact, it was two years after her coming that the reaping took place. The month was November, and Grandma was with us on one of her frequent visits.

We were in the sitting room that evening, Grandma, my parents and I, when the doorbell rang and, a moment later,

114

Jeanie Bronach-Kerr came in. Jeanie was nearly twenty now and as different from her mother as morning from night; a slender girl of medium height with gentle blue-grey eyes and a warm winning smile. Unlike her mother, she cherished no illusions of superiority and, within 'the limits of convention and propriety, was disposed to be friendly with everyone. For a year now, since leaving finishing school, she had found occupation in church work and in that time she and my mother had become close friends.

"It's about Mr. Calder's retirement gift, Jess," she said as she seated herself. "They've decided on a silver service and I'm helping with the collecting."

My mother nodded. "He deserves it," she said. "He's had the pulpit ever since I was a wee girl." She half-closed her eyes, doing some rapid mental arithmetic. "About ten shillings, Jeanie?"

"That's what most of them are giving." Jeanie took a small note book from her handbag. "Will I put you down for that?"

"All right." My mother looked at my father. "Cough up, Robert."

Looking slightly pained, my father coughed up.

Grandma, who had been watching Jeanie's face with sharp grey eyes, spoke suddenly:

"Lassie, you're not lookin' up to your usual. Do you need a tonic?"

"I don't think so, Mrs. Guthrie." Jeanie flushed slightly. "I feel quite well."

My mother was looking at her now with new intentness. "Are you sure, Jeanie? I don't want to frighten you, but you do seem a little peaky."

"I'm all right, Jess." Jeanie got up suddenly, and I saw that her mouth was trembling. "I must get along," she said with difficulty. "Good-bye, Mrs. Guthrie . . . Mr. Mackinley."

Before my father could rise, she opened the door and went out, and after a momentary hesitation, my mother got up and followed her. For five minutes the murmur of their voices came from the hall, and then the front door closed and my mother came back. Her eyes, I saw with surprise, were bright with tears.

"The utterly horrible creature!" she said with anger and distress. "Do you know what she's done?"

"Jeanie?" my father said, incredulity in his voice.

"No, no! Mrs. Bronach-Kerr. Somehow, she heard about Peter's father being a blacksmith and she's broken the engagement. No wonder Jeanie looked peaky!"

"Great Scott!" I saw the echo of her distress in my father's eyes. "How could she? And them so daft about each other."

"Peter?" said Grandma. "What Peter's this?"

"Oh, you know, Mamma — Peter Glennie. You met him here last spring. Born in Kilbrannon but came here from a Glasgow paper to take an editorship with the West-Scotland Weekly."

"Aye, to be sure," said Grandma. "I mind now. A real likely callant. So he and Jeanie are in love?"

"In love!" my mother said. "Mad about each other. And so happy with each other. Oh, that woman! I could — could scratch her eyes out."

"The very thing!" said Grandma with sarcasm. "No, Jessie, we'll have to do better than that."

"That's just it, Mamma — there's nothing we can do."

"Havers!" snapped Grandma. "There's aye a way out if a body'll just look for it."

"Not in this case," my father said. "If Mrs. Bronach-Kerr's made up her mind that Peter's beneath her, it would be impossible to change her."

"Impossible!" Grandma snorted. "The most ridiculous word in the Scottish language. She can be changed. Aye, and with the Lord's help, I'm the one that'll do it."

My mother was looking at her, half-hopefully, half-doubtingly. "How, Mamma?"

"Don't speir me, Jessie," said Grandma testily. "The woman's a snob, and because she's a snob I'll have my way with her. But don't ask me how. I've got to think it over." . . .

After dinner that same evening, I saw that instead of knitting, Grandma had dug up some old copies of the West-Scotland Weekly and was poring over them. Presently she laid them aside and looked across at my mother.

"Jessie, this series of articles on 'Old Ayrshire Families' —who gets them up?"

116

"Peter Glennie," my mother said. "Why, Mamma?"
Grandma's eyes had turned hard and bright. "Because
I was hopin' that would be the way of it," she said and picked
up her knitting. And, knowing her, none of us pressed her
further. . . .

But it was evident from then on that Grandma had
evolved some plan to help Jeanie and Peter Glennie. She
began to absent herself from the house, sometimes for an
afternoon, sometimes for a whole day, and once, even, for
overnight. But what all this gadding about meant she was
careful not to enlighten us.

On a Thursday afternoon about ten days later we were
at tea when Grandma, who had been away all day, arrived
and sat down with us. She was, for her, in high good humour,
addressing my father with dour jocularity as "ma mannie" and
my mother as "ma bonnie wean." Afterward, when Mary
had cleared away, she took a penny exercise book and a sheaf
of papers from her handbag and laid them on the table.

"Your pen, ma mannie," she said to my father.

Not without reluctance, I noted, my father handed her his
precious fountain pen (something of a novelty in those days)
and then sat watching her as she began to write in the exercise
book.

"I suppose," he said at last, "it would be quite useless to
ask you what you're doing?"

"Not at all, Robert," said Grandma austerely. "I'm jottin'
down the makin's of a history of the Bronach family."

There was a brief startled silence.

"The Bronach family!" my mother exclaimed. "Good
gracious, Mamma, what for?"

"What else for but to give to Peter Glennie? They're an
old Ayrshire family and without a doubt he'd be interested."

"So that's it?" There was a chill of disapproval in my
father's voice. "Well, I'm afraid you're wasting your time.
Peter'll never soften Mrs. Bronach-Kerr up that way."

"You tell me so, Robert?" Grandma's nostrils were
flaring. "Well, I'll remind you of that remark in a day or two."
She turned to my mother. "By the way, Jessie, I want you to
have the Glennie lad in some evenin' soon. You can mention
that I'd like a word with him."

117

"I'll try, Mamma. What do you want to see him for?"

"Ask your man, there," said Grandma, and returned to her writing. "He'll tell you all about it." . . .

A prompt acceptance of my mother's invitation came from Mr. Glennie in the next afternoon's mail, and that evening after dinner we sat waiting with varying degrees and qualities of expectation for him to appear. At last the doorbell rang and Mary ushered him into the sitting room. He was tall and compactly built, with a lean dark face, a shock of black hair, glistening now from the brush, and friendly, if rather melancholy, brown eyes.

Greetings over, he dropped to a place on the sofa beside my mother and for a little there was the usual desultory talk. Then there was a pause, and my father looked across at Grandma, anticipation in his face.

"Well," he said smoothly, "I believe you have something to say to Peter."

"Quite right, Robert." Grandma gave a little sniff and rose. "But not here," she said, and stalked over to the door of the little anteroom that my mother kept for a sewing room. "In here, laddie," she commanded. "I hope you have a match to light the gas."

A light went on in the sewing room and the door closed. My mother turned to my father with raised eyebrows.

He grinned. " 'Let not thy left hand know what thy right hand doeth.' That's your mother, Jess."

"But, Robert, we know what she's doing."

"I wonder?" He stroked his cheek reflectively. "It's not like her to pander to Mrs. Bronach-Kerr's snobbishness, even for the sake of Jeanie and Peter. Yet what other answer is there?"

It was half an hour later when the sewing-room door opened and Grandma and Mr. Glennie came out. Grandma's face was grim and inscrutable as always, but I saw that the melancholy had cleared from Mr. Glennie's eyes and that they were alight from some inner excitement. Apparently, however, he had been well briefed by Grandma, for throughout the rest of the evening he made no slightest reference to what had passed in the sewing room.

118

Later, though, just as he was on the point of leaving, Grandma got up and went over to the door.

"Laddie, you'll let me know what happens? If anythin' does happen."

"Of course, Mrs. Guthrie." He smiled into her grim old face, almost with affection. "And thank you, anyway. Ever so much."

On Monday afternoon I had got back early from school and was in the sitting room with my mother when Grandma came in, dressed for outdoors: an austere and imposing figure in the unrelieved black of her widowhood.

"I expect to be back for tea, Jessie," she said. "But if I'm late mind and keep the teapot on the hob for me."

"Yes, Mamma. But where are you going?"

Grandma's eyes glinted. "I'm goin' callin' on Mrs. Bronach-Kerr."

"What!" My mother sat up. "But, Mamma, you don't know each other."

"No, but we're going' to," said Grandma. "And I'm hopin' it'll profit us both."

I was afire with curiosity. As she marched out through the hall and down the front steps, I followed her.

"Grandma," I begged, "can I go with you?"

She wheeled about and then stood eyeing me with dour thoughtfulness. "Aye," she muttered, "where I know nothin' about the woman, a witness mightn't come amiss." She turned again. "Come on, then."

The old Harvey place, a two-and-a-half storey pile of grey sandstone, was only a three-minute walk from home. As we turned in at the double gateway and walked up the drive, a curtain in one of the bay windows moved, and I guessed that we were under observation. At the entrance Grandma tugged vigorously at the bell pull, and after a brief wait a smartly uniformed maid looked out at us.

"Yes, ma'am?"

"I'm Mrs. Guthrie," said Grandma. "Will you be good enough to tell your mistress that I'd like a word with her?"

"I'm sorry, ma'am. Mrs. Bronach-Kerr's not at home."

"None of your fibs, girl!" said Grandma sternly. "Did I not see her myself, keekin' at me from behind the window curtain?"

119

Flushing, the maid glanced over her shoulder. "I wasna fibbin'," she whispered. "That's what she makes me say when she doesna want to see anybody."

Grandma's tongue clicked. "The idea! Well, away you in and tell her I know she's at home and want to see her."

The maid hesitated and then left us. In a little while she was back.

"She'll see ye," she said in an undertone. "But it's a wonder."

The room we were ushered into was spacious, richly carpeted, and furnished with a divan and deep over-stuffed chairs that were in marked contrast to the severe horsehair of my own home. By a high ornate mantel Mrs. Bronach-Kerr was standing, cold eyes watching us along the bridge of her nose.

Grandma introduced herself. "You'll know my daughter, Mrs. Robert Mackinley," she added.

Mrs. Bronach-Kerr's eyebrows lifted slightly. "I've seen Mrs. Mackinley, I believe," she said without enthusiasm. "In church."

I heard Grandma give a soft, almost inaudible snort.

"My reason for callin'," she said: "I've been engaged this while back in gettin' up a short history of the Bronach family of Ayrshire, and I concluded it might pay me to talk it over with you."

"Oh, really?" Mrs. Bronach-Kerr thawed perceptibly. "How very interesting. I've always meant to look into my ancestry but never got around to it."

"A pity," said Grandma. "There have been some notable Bronachs in the past." And I wondered at a certain dryness in her voice.

"Yes, I can believe that," Mrs. Bronach-Kerr said. "My father, you know, was an extremely clever and capable person, and I do think that heredity tells." Her hand moved in a gesture that included me. "But won't you sit down?"

I chose one of the deep chairs and was almost engulfed in its soft yielding interior. Grandma, however, drew a straight chair away from the wall and lowered herself stiffly to its edge.

"Now." Mrs. Bronach-Kerr sank down on the divan. "Just what can I do for you, Mrs. Guthrie?"

120

"I'll tell you." Grandma took the exercise book from her handbag and opened it. "On searchin' back I find that the first of the Ayrshire Bronachs was one Thomas Bronach who drifted into these parts around 1660 and settled near Fernie. All the archives tell about him, however, is that he was a farm labourer. Have you ever heard tell of him?"

"Mrs. Guthrie, this is preposterous. You must have made a mistake."

"I'm afraid not." Some of the chill had come back to Mrs. Bronach-Kerr's voice. "Are you quite sure you have the right Bronach?"

"Positive," said Grandma. "I've traced the direct line from Thomas to your father." She turned a page. "Thomas' son, also Thomas, seems to have followed in his father's footsteps, but his son, Andrew, was a man of some note. Andrew, it seems, was a tinker and a hard-workin' man, but he had a vile temper and in the year 1731 he was hanged for murderin' his wife."

121

Mrs. Bronach-Kerr was staring at her, dismay on her face. "Mrs. Guthrie, this is preposterous. You must have made a mistake."

"No," said Grandma firmly. "There's no mistake. It's all there in the records." She turned another page or two. "But to get on: The next two generations of Bronachs were nothin' outstandin' — just honest decent workin' men. Then we come to your great-great-grandfather, John Bronach. John seems to have been a fella of some enterprise, for in 1805 he contrived to open a tavern at Port Auchter, patronized by sailors and the riff-raff of the town. For ten years he did very well, then the excise people discovered he was smugglin' in a good part of the drink he sold, and he had to flee the country, leavin' behind him in poverty a wife and a son."

A stifled exclamation came from Mrs. Bronach-Kerr, and I saw that she was sitting bolt upright on the divan, distended eyes on Grandma's face.

"The son," went on Grandma calmly, "was your great-grandfather, Timothy, twenty-five at the time. And, poor fella, he seems to have had a hard time of it. He had taken as his common-law wife one of his father's barmaids, and now, left penniless and with a bairn of his own to raise, he struggled along for a time and then took to drink. Tipsy Tim, he was known as in Port Auchter—"

"Stop!" Mrs. Bronach-Kerr was on her feet, her face crimson. "I refuse to listen. This whole thing is nothing but a deliberate and malicious fabrication."

Grandma shook her head sombrely. "It's the truth, you poor creature, as you well know. And a bitter pill, I can see. But don't lose sight of the fact that it's not the whole truth, for it takes no stock of scores of other Bronach descendants who might well be famous for all I know."

But apparently this was no comfort to Mrs. Bronach-Kerr. Her hands clenched at her sides, she paced across the room and then came back to Grandma.

"Mrs. Guthrie," she said, her voice high and shaken, "what do you intend to do with this—this history?"

"It's early to say," said Grandma. "So far, I've only talked it over with one editor."

Mrs. Bronach-Kerr gasped. "What editor?"

"Mr. Peter Glennie of the West-Scotland Weekly."

Something like horror came into Mrs. Bronach-Kerr's face. "Peter Glennie! So that's it! He put you up to this. This is his revenge—"

"He did not," snapped Grandma. "He knew nothin' whatever about it till I showed it to him."

"But he'll buy it, knowing it will injure me. Because it will injure me."

"You're mistaken," said Grandma. "He said he wouldn't think of publishin' it."

Mrs. Bronach-Kerr's eyes distended. "He—he wouldn't!"

"Aye, just that. Which was exactly what I'd expected. A fine lad, and a decent lad, Peter Glennie. Like your father, he was born of humble parents but by sheer ability has made somethin' of himself. If you respect your father, you can't but respect Peter, too."

Mrs. Bronach-Kerr was staring at her. "Mrs. Guthrie," she said, and dropped back on the divan, "will you tell me just why you came here today?"

"I've as good as told you," said Grandma. "I'm here in the interests of two young people who love each other dearly but who're barred from findin' happiness in marriage." She tapped the exercise book. "And for no good reason at all, as you must now be able to see."

Again color swept into Mrs. Bronach-Kerr's face. "I believed I had a reason. I—I had no idea—" She got up suddenly and went over to the window. For a little she stood there, her back to us, and then turned. "Mrs. Guthrie, will you give me a little time to think about all this? It's been—well, rather a shock, and I'd like to adjust myself before making any decisions."

"Very well, ma'am." Grandma stood up, and I knew that she was disappointed. "Then I'll leave you to do your thinkin'."

"Wait!" Mrs. Bronach-Kerr came over from the window. "But what about the history? If it were published, it would be simply —Mrs. Guthrie, would you sell it to me?"

Grandma eyed her cannily. "I'd prefer not," she said. "However, while you're makin' up your mind about Peter and Jeanie, I'll think it over." She bowed stiffly. "I wish you a good day, ma'am . . . Come, Duncan." . . .

123

My father was home when we got back to the house. As we sat down to tea I saw that he was studying Grandma's expressionless face with frank curiosity. Finally, he could contain himself no longer.

"I trust," he said suavely, "that Mrs. Bronach-Kerr was suitably grateful to Peter for publishing the history of her family?"

Grandma gave a little grunt. "Ask me no questions, Robert, and I'll tell you no lies. In a day or two you'll know all about it, so just possess your soul in patience."

But it was to be much sooner than that. That evening after dinner we were in the sitting room when the doorbell pealed lustily and Peter and Jeanie burst in on us, their faces radiant.

"Look!" Peter held aloft Jeanie's left hand on which a diamond sparkled in the gaslight. "We're engaged again!"

"Engaged again!" echoed my father. "Great Scott, then it did work!"

But my mother had sprung from her chair and was hugging Jeanie, her eyes brimming with tears.

"Oh, I'm so glad for you, dear! So glad for you both!"

"Thanks, Jess." Her mouth trembling, Jeanie turned and let my father wring her hand. "I can hardly believe it," she faltered. "It's like a—like a miracle."

And then she left them and went over to Grandma, who had risen and was watching the scene, dourly but with a glint of satisfaction in her eyes.

"And we owe it all to you, Mrs. Guthrie," she said with feeling. "You're the one we have to thank." Before Grandma could stop her, she threw her arms around the old lady's neck and kissed her warmly.

Flustered, Grandma released herself, though not ungently. "Such a to-do!" she sputtered. "Lassie, if you feel you must thank somebody, then the Lord's the one for you to thank. I'm only His handmaiden."

Peter had come over to Jeanie's side.

"Mrs. Guthrie," he said, "I have a message for you. From Jeanie's mother."

"Aye?" Grandma's eyes sharpened. "What is't, laddie?"

"I'm to tell you," said Peter, "that she agrees with what

124

you said this afternoon and that she is giving her permission to our marriage regardless of anything you may do with the history of her family."

"Well, good for her!" said Grandma. "I'd a notion she'd try to bargain with me. It just shows that under this dreich nonsense of hers she's a decent enough body."

"Just the same, Mrs. Guthrie," Jeanie said pleadingly, "she's badly worried about the history. It was quite a blow to learn that there had been so many disreputable Bronachs, and after the way she has acted, it would be humiliating if it were published."

Behind me I heard my father give a soft exclamation.

"As if any editor in his right mind would think of such a thing!" said Grandma. "However, we'll just set her mind at rest." She went over to her handbag and came back with the exercise book. "Here, lassie," she said, and handed it to Jeanie. "Give this to your mother with my compliments. Aye, and with my respects."

"Oh, thank you!" Jeanie blinked moisture from her eyes. "This makes everything perfect. How am I ever to thank you, Mrs. Guthrie?"

"How, indeed?" said Peter fervently. "If it hadn't been for you, Mrs. Guthrie—"

"Ach, wheest!" said Grandma testily. "Wheest, the both of you! I would think, newly engaged as you are, that you'd have better to do than pester an old woman."

So after a little the happy couple left, and we settled down again in the sitting room.

"Well, Robert?" said Grandma with significance.

My father grimaced. "Oh, I know. I owe you an apology. It never occurred to me that you might be getting at her that way."

"Save your apology, my mannie," said Grandma. "You thought just what I wanted you to think, and I've had my fun off you and that wife of yours."

"But, Mamma," my mother said, "what I don't understand is how you knew that Mrs. Bronach-Kerr's ancestry was so spotty."

Grandma sighed. "My, Jessie, but it's the simple soul you

125

are. Do you not know that in all the length and breadth of the land there's not a family that hasn't its skeleton or two?"

"I suppose so," my mother said slowly. "And as it happened, Mrs. Bronach-Kerr's family was full of them?"

"It was not," said Grandma. "It was full of decent workin' men. They only looked like skeletons because the woman's a snob." She added after a little pause. "Or was a snob. Poor creature, this'll have been an eye-opener to her."

Which, as Mrs. Bronach-Kerr's subsequent conduct proved, was indeed the case.

GRANDMA
... and the Misogamist

WHEN MY father got back from Dumfries after the funeral of his Aunt Maria, a spinster of sixty-some years, it was no great surprise to find him rather quiet and subdued. With the Scottish Presbyterians of fifty years ago, a funeral was a heart-chilling, almost macabre, occasion — the grim black coffin and its pallid occupant; the long pessimistic funeral service, which left the hearer wondering depressedly at which of two possible destinations the departed soul had arrived; the slow dragging walk, or ride, to the cemetery, and for a finale, the haunting thump-thump of the first clods on the coffin top.

Even after tea, when food and drink should have restored his good spirits, he sat by the fire, the paper unopened on his knee, frowning into the flames, and from time to time I saw my mother glance at him with something between concern and perplexity in her eyes. Finally, she went over and sat on the arm of his chair, her arm around his shoulders.

"Don't think about it, dear," she said gently. "After all, she's at rest now. And it's not as if you had ever been very close to her."

My father shook his head. "It's not Aunt Maria I'm thinking about, Jess. It's Uncle Ronald."

"Oh? Is he poorly?"

"No, not at all. He's fine. But the thing is, now he's

alone in the world, I've got better than a notion we'll be having him here."

"Well, why not. After all, poor old man, with his sister just gone, it's only natural he'd come to stay with us for a while."

"That's just it, Jess. It wouldn't be for a while; it would be for the rest of his days. He as good as said so."

I saw consternation come to life in my mother's face. "But, Robert, where's the need of that? He'll be well off now with Aunt Maria's income on top of his own and able to afford a housekeeper. Or he might even marry."

"Never that," my father said. "He's bitterly opposed to marriage. Aunt Maria's doing, of course. She was always frightened he'd take a wife and leave her alone and she systematically poisoned him against marriage. Nor would he have a housekeeper. He'd be too frightened she might trick him into marrying her." He looked up at her, regret in his eyes. "I'm awful sorry, Jess. It'll mean more work for you, but I couldn't very well tell him to stay away."

"Of course not." My mother patted his cheek. "And don't worry about the work. As for his making his home with us—well, we'll just wait and see what he's like. If he's the right kind it may work out very well."

One afternoon about a week later I came home from school and heard voices in the sitting room. Curious, I slipped along the hall and peeped in the doorway. My mother was sitting on the sofa, her hands folded formally in her lap, and opposite her, in my father's chair, there was a little wizened man with a shock of bristling grey hair. His deeply lined face was mild, almost timid, in expression, but with an underlying stubbornness I could feel, rather than see.

As though sensing my presence, my mother turned and then beckoned to me. "Come away in, Duncan. I want you to meet your Uncle Ronald."

I went in and shook a bony but limp hand.

"So this is Duncan?" Uncle Ronald said with no great warmth. He looked at me uneasily. "A big strappin' laddie. You'll have a sling, I suppose, Duncan?"

I shook my head, wondering at the question. "No, Uncle Ronald. I had one but it got broken."

"But you'll have a pea-shooter, belike? Or maybe one of these air guns?"

"No, I haven't," I said. "Father says I'm too wee yet to have an air gun."

"He's a wise man," Uncle Ronald said with relief in his voice. He turned to my mother. "I'm kinda feared o' laddies, Jessie. Wee rascals, aye pappin' peas or stones or things at you, or roarin' and shoutin' and racin' about. I hope Duncan's not a noisy boy?"

"He's no noisier than most," my mother said, a little stiffly. "I'd be worried about him if he was quiet."

"To be sure, Jessie," Uncle Ronald said placatingly. "I wasn't findin' fault with him. He's a braw laddie, I can see, and I'm sure we're going to be the best o' friends."

Personally, I doubted it. Already I had a feeling that as long as Uncle Ronald was with us I was going to find restrictions placed on my personal freedom.

I was only too right. Uncle Ronald may have been timid and unassertive, but he had a way of making his wishes known and having them observed, and I soon found that he had become a repressive influence in my life.

As before, I was allowed to sing and whistle around the house, but not in the same room with Uncle Ronald and never when he was taking one of the several naps that, he said, were essential to his well-being. It was impressed on me, also, that I must close doors gently, not slam them; that I must walk, not run, up and down stairs; and that any activity productive of noise must be conducted in the storeroom or out in the coal shed. Life with Uncle Ronald, it seemed to me, was a dreary business.

Mary Strachan, our maid, detested him. Uncle Ronald, whose room was at the back of the house, next to hers, evinced a sudden desire for a different bedroom, and when Mary discovered that the change, with all the extra work entailed, was on account of her snoring, she could hardly contain her indignation. "Fuithery auld pest!" I heard her mutter once when Uncle Ronald hinted gently that his hot-water bottle could be hotter than had been the case in the past. "A body would think it was a hotel we was runnin'."

Nor were my parents in much better case. Once, after my father had reproved me for tinkling at the piano while

129

Uncle Ronald was napping, I overheard my mother say, "Really, Robert, it's not fair. This is Duncan's home but he's not at home in it any longer. In fact, none of us are."

"You needn't tell me," my father said unhappily. "But, Jess, he's only been here three weeks. Let's give him a little longer before we do anything."

So Uncle Ronald stayed on. Then, suddenly, the situation changed, and for the worse. Uncle Ronald developed sciatica and was confined, groaning and complaining, to his bed.

Beyond keeping him warm and comfortable as possible, the doctor said, there was little to be done but let the sciatica run its course. He left some phenacetin-and-caffein powders to help ease the pain and promised to send a bottle of embrocation from the chemist's in town.

When he had gone my parents looked at each other, their faces expressive.

"A fine do," my father said ruefully. "What do we do now?"

"We get him a nurse," my mother said flatly. "There's enough work here for Mary and me without having an invalid on our hands."

My father shook his head forebodingly. "I doubt he'll like that, lass."

"He'll have to like it, Robert. I don't mean to be unkind, and I am sorry for him, but you'll have to make him understand that it's a nurse or go to a hospital. Gracious, think of the extra work—keeping a fire in his room, serving his meals, giving him his medicine and rubbing his leg and attending to all his other needs. I refuse to even attempt it."

"I see your point," my father said docilely. "Well, I'll tell him."

He went up to Uncle Ronald's room, and my mother and I waited in the sitting room for the verdict. It was nearly half an hour before he came back, and I saw that he was frowning.

"Well?" my mother said anxiously. "What did he say?"

My father grimaced. "What did he not say! He was real put out at first, but I managed to convince him finally he ought to have a nurse. But it's got to be an elderly and responsible woman. None of these flighty flirty young baggages, if you please."

130

My mother's tongue clicked. "Ridiculous! However, you've won your point, so—"

"Hold on, now," my father said. "I didn't have it all my own way, by any means. He'll have a nurse, and he'll pay her wages, but he insists that she live in so she'll be available night or day."

My mother gave a moan of dismay. "Oh, my gracious! That'll leave me with only Mamma's room vacant. What if we have company?"

"I'm afraid we'll just have to chance that, Jess. Surely his sciatica will not last more than a week or two?"

"I most sincerely hope not," my mother said. "Well, now, what about a nurse?"

"You have nobody in mind?"

"Yes, I have. You know that Mrs. O'Toole that lost her husband last year? Well, she goes out nursing now and should be just the person—about fifty, very capable and a kindly good-natured soul, I hear."

"She'll need to be," my father said. "Uncle Ronald'll expect his full money's worth. I'll take a daunder in to town after dinner and see if she's free."

Mrs. O'Toole arrived the next morning and without loss of time took over the care of Uncle Ronald. As my mother had said, she was kindly and good-natured, a plump, still comely woman with soft brown eyes and a quick jolly laugh. And, to our surprise, far from finding Uncle Ronald a trial, she seemed actually to enjoy looking after him.

"My," she observed to my mother, "he's such a nice wee man. Sae gentle and couthie, in spite of all his sufferin'. What way did he never get married?"

"He never got the chance," my mother said. "For most of his life he was under the influence of an older sister, an embittered old maid, and she turned him against marriage."

"Och, the wretch!" said Mrs. O'Toole indignantly. "What a black burnin' shame! And him just the one tae make some lucky woman happy!"

Later, my mother reported this conversation to my father. "So you see," she said with a giggle, "if Uncle Ronald wants a wife all he has to do is say the word."

My father grunted. "I can hear him," he said with

131

irony. "Mrs. O'Toole would be wise not to get her hopes built up." . . .

It was a full month before Uncle Ronald was able to leave his bed. And now my mother began to look forward to getting one of her spare rooms back. But though another week found the invalid coming down for his meals, he still said nothing about letting Mrs. O'Toole go.

"Why on earth is he keeping her?" my mother said when still another week slid by. "He doesn't need her now."

"No," my father said, "but he enjoys having her. Look at the way she pampers him, at his beck and call any hour of the day or night. He's never been made so much of in all his life."

"Then I should think he'd want to marry her."

"Not him. He's perfectly content with things as they are."

"Well, I'm not," my mother blazed suddenly. "If he was poor it would be a different story, but as it is he's just abusing our hospitality, and it's high time you did something, Robert."

My father looked at her with awe. It was a rare thing to see my mother really angry. "What do you want me to do, Jess?"

"I want you to tell him to let Mrs. O'Toole go; that we need the room she's occupying."

"All right." My father sighed. "It's a hard thing, but I'll do it."

My mother's face softened. "Don't feel so cast down about it, dear. Who knows, maybe losing Mrs. O'Toole will be enough to induce him to marry her."

"Maybe," said my father. "And maybe I'll grow wings and fly to the moon."

When my father came down from this second interview with Uncle Ronald he was seriously upset.

"My conscience!" he groaned. "If there's one thing I cannot abide it's a man that greets."

"Greets?" my mother said. "Well, I hope you didn't let his tears wash away your resolve?"

"I did not. Mrs. O'Toole is going. But, my, Jess, if you could have heard him! I felt like a butcher."

Mrs. O'Toole left the next day. In tears. And for a solid week Uncle Ronald spoke to none of us. But if he was annoyed, he wasn't sufficiently annoyed to do anything about leaving, and as the weeks slid by I could see that my mother's patience was wearing thin. Finally, one evening when Uncle Ronald had retired, after suggesting mildly that he'd appreciate quiet in the house, her patience snapped.

"I'm not going to put up with this any longer," she declared. "I'd be just as happy living in a morgue. Uncle Ronald has a house of his own in Dumfries, and if he won't have a housekeeper he can at least get a manservant of some kind. But he's going. You tell him so, Robert."

"I can't, Jess," my father said wretchedly. "It was bad enough when I made him let Mrs. O'Toole go. Dear knows what he'd do if I told him he had to get out."

"And what about me and Duncan? Are we to go on forever being strangers in our own home?"

"Of course not, lass. But just hang on a while. Something'll turn up."

"No doubt," my mother said coldly. "We'll all go stark staring mad and that'll be the end of it."

But a week or so later something did turn up: Grandma arrived on one of her periodic visits.

It was a Saturday afternoon and my father was home, Uncle Ronald up in his room, napping.

"My, but I'm glad to see you," my father said with unusual warmth, as we settled down in the sitting room. "You're like an answer to prayer."

If Grandma was gratified at this cordial reception, her face, grim and unsmiling as always, failed to show it. "Aye, I know all about it," she said. "I got Jessie's last letter yesterday and concluded I'd better come and see for myself what kind of habble it is you're in." She eyed us over her knitting. "You're all lookin' well enough, at least."

"We are well," my mother said. "Or as well as can be expected."

"Gracious!" said Grandma. "Lassie, you sound as if you were at a funeral."

"I am," my mother said bitterly. "The funeral of our happy family life. And Uncle Ronald's the undertaker."

"Still here, is he?"

"Of course. Robert enjoys his company too much to let him go."

133

"Jess!" my father protested. "That's not fair. You know fine that, short of being brutal, there's nothing to be done."

"Havers, Robert!" said Grandma. "To hear you, a body would think there was no Lord in His heaven. There's aye somethin' to be done."

"What?" My father looked at her hopefully.

"I can't tell you, Robert," said Grandma. "Not till I've met Mr. Mackinley. And maybe I'll not tell you then."

The meeting of Grandma and Uncle Ronald took place just before tea. It was impossible to tell from her face what she thought of him, but there was no mistaking how Uncle Ronald felt about her. He was scared to death of her. So much so, in fact, that right after tea, on a plea of weariness, he fled back to the sanctuary of his room.

"My faith!" said Grandma as the door closed on him. "He must have taken me for Auld Hornie. What a scairt thrawn wee creature!"

"Well?" My father was eyeing her hopefully again. "Do you know now what to do?"

"Aye, Robert. I think so."

"What?"

Grandma shook her head. "You'll see when the time comes. But it's very simple."

"Simple?" My father frowned. "You're not proposing to just throw him out?"

"Don't be daft, man!" snapped Grandma. "I said simple, not stupid. Mr. Mackinley'll leave here gladly and without ill-will toward either of you." She turned to my mother, and I knew by the flaring of her nostrils that something was amusing her. "Jessie, have you noticed Mr. Mackinley's resemblance to your father?"

"To Father?" My mother looked at her with surprise. "Well, hardly. Unless, perhaps, in his general appearance. But he's not anything like Father, really."

"I didn't say he was, Jessie. But I was real taken with him, just the same. A timid and blate wee soul, but good and decent and civil. To say nothing of bein' well-to-do. Just the kind a lonely woman like me would want for companionship in her last days."

"Good gracious!" my mother exclaimed. "Mamma, what are you hinting at?"

134

"Who's hintin'?" demanded Grandma. "I'm tellin' you."

"But, Mamma, surely this isn't your simple solution — marrying him?"

"What way not, may I inquire?" said Grandma acidly, although, knowing her so well, I had a feeling she was enjoying herself. "Would that not solve your problem?"

"Well, I—I suppose it would. But he wouldn't do it. If he wouldn't marry Mrs. O'Toole, he certainly—" My mother stopped abruptly, her face colouring.

"Aye, my bonnie?" said Grandma with icy blandness. "You were sayin'?"

My father came to the rescue. "She means that Uncle Ronald has always been strongly opposed to marriage and wouldn't have anybody for his wife."

"That shows he's normal," said Grandma. "With most of men, gettin' married is like a cold plunge—they hold back till they get pushed in, and then they find it's not so bad. Look at Robert, there."

"Yes," my father grinned, "but I'm not Uncle Ronald. He's far too canny to get pushed in. You'll never do it."

"Maybe not, ma mannie," said Grandma. "But I'll promise you this: If I don't push him in, it'll not be from lack of tryin'."

My mother was staring at her. "Mamma, you don't mean it? Not really? This is just a joke."

"It's no joke," said Grandma firmly. "I was never more serious in my life. If you doubt it, just wait and see what happens."

It happened, or began to happen, right after we got back from kirk the next evening. Uncle Ronald, who had been prevailed upon to accompany us, was on the point of scuttling off to his room when Grandma stopped him.

"Wait a wee, Mr. Mackinley," she ordered. "Come in the sittin' room with us. I have something to say to you."

Uncle Ronald cast a look of longing at the stairway and then, with obvious reluctance, joined us in the sitting room.

"Now, tell me this," said Grandma when we were seated: "How old are you?"

Uncle Ronald, who was watching her uneasily, gave a start of surprise. "How old? I'm sixty-one past, Mrs. Guthrie."

"For marriage, of course. What else?"

"Fine," said Grandma. "Just my own age—or near enough."

"Near enough for what, ma'am?"

"For marriage, of course. What else?"

My mother had turned crimson. "Mamma! For mercy's sake—"

"That'll do you, Jessie," said Grandma sternly. "You'll be good enough to let me conduct my affairs in my own way." She turned back to Uncle Ronald. "I've been thinkin' it over and have finally made up my mind—the best thing for two lonely old bodies like you and me is to get married. You can see that, Mr. Mackinley—or, since we're as good as engaged—Ronald?"

Uncle Ronald's eyes were almost popping from his head. "But I don't want to get married," he quavered.

"What!" Grandma scowled at him menacingly. "You're not goin' to tell me you're too good for me?"

"N-no," faltered Uncle Ronald. "Oh, no. It's just that I'm not good enough for you."

"Aye, true," said Grandma. "But I'm democratic and I'll not be stickin'. The main thing is that it's to both our advantages to get married. Anybody can see with half an eye that what you need is a good strong active intelligent woman to look after you and give you an interest in life—"

"But I don't need lookin' after," Uncle Ronald said with desperation. "I can look after myself—"

"Wheest!" snapped Grandma. "That's somethin' you'll have to learn, Ronald—not to interrupt me. It's ill-mannered. Now, we'll take my side of it: I've often thought it would be a good thing if I kept a few hens down at my place in Ardrach, but I'm away so much, it's aye been out of the question. But it'll be easy once we're married. You'll be there then to feed the hens, and maybe a hutchful of rabbits—braw eatin', for a change, rabbit. And we'll have a kale yard and grow our own vegetables. Fine exercise for a man, a kale yard. All the diggin' and rakin' and plantin'. It'll make a new man of you, Ronald. Tell me, have you ever milked a coo?"

Uncle Ronald had risen and was standing half crouched, his face full of a kind of horror. "Mrs. Guthrie, I—I appreciate the honor you do me, but I don't—"

137

"I'm glad to hear it, Ronald. It's a promisin' sign for the future."

"But—you don't understand—"

"Not another cheep out of you!" barked Grandma. "I can see you're grateful, but there's no need to go on about it. In the mornin' I'll away in to town and make the necessary arrangements and we'll get married—Here! Where are you off to? Come back, Ronald!"

But Uncle Ronald was gone, in full flight to his room.

My father was watching Grandma, vexation in his eyes. "So that's what you're after?" he said. "Well, it may be very simple, but it seems to me you might as well throw him out of the house as frighten him out of it."

"Don't blether, Robert!" snapped Grandma. "You know me better than that. I told you it was marriage I was after, and I meant it."

"Then you ought to be ashamed of yourself," my mother said with more heat than discretion. "I never was so mortified in my life."

To my surprise, Grandma took no offence. "You'll get over it, Jessie," she said equably. "Just wait till you get some of the braw vegetables from my husband's kale yard." . . .

After breakfast next morning, from which Uncle Ronald was absent, Grandma got ready to go in to town.

"Jessie," she said before leaving, "you'll tell Ronald that he's not to try runnin' away, for if he does I'll just come after him."

"I will not," my mother said rebelliously. "I'll have nothing to do with this disgraceful business."

"A pity," murmured Grandma with unwonted mildness. "Such a trauchle havin' to lock the creature in his room."

"Oh, goodness gracious!" my mother said faintly. "All right, Mamma. I'll tell him."

I was just leaving for school when Uncle Ronald came creeping downstairs, driven, I suppose, by hunger. Blushing and stammering, my mother gave him Grandma's message, and I guessed from the dismay in his face that flight was exactly what he had been contemplating.

"Oh, dear!" he quavered. "Jessie, what am I to do?"

My mother looked at him with pity. "There's just one

138

way, Uncle Ronald," she said gently: "Tell her, plump and plain, that you want nothing to do with her. After all, she can't force you to marry her."

"Oh, I couldn't do that!" gasped Uncle Ronald. "I wouldn't dare."

My mother sighed. "Then the next best thing is to stay in your room till she leaves. I'll see that Mary brings you your meals." . . .

When I came home at noon I found Grandma out in the kitchen with Mary. They were deep in conversation, but broke off as I came through the doorway.

"So there you are, my wee mannie," said Grandma. "Now, you wash your hands at the job-box and we'll have a bite to eat."

I obeyed. But as I did so I wondered what Grandma had been saying to Mary and why Mary had been giggling. . . .

We went in to lunch, Grandma, my mother and I, and were about halfway through when my mother straightened suddenly.

"Listen!" she said, her head tipped on one side.

Grandma looked at her quickly. "Listen to what?" she said loudly. "What is it you think you hear, Jessie?" Almost, it seemed to me, as if the words were intended for ears other than my mother's.

My mother gave a little frown of annoyance. "Gracious, Mamma, surely you don't need to shout? It's funny, but it was as if there was somebody in the house. I thought I heard whispering."

"Did you, now?" said Grandma. "Wouldn't it be Mary?"

"Maybe." My mother returned to her lunch. "Or maybe I just imagined it."

But I knew she hadn't imagined it. I, too, had heard whispering, but something told me I would be wise to hold my tongue. . . .

When I got home in the afternoon Grandma and my mother were in the sitting room. Grandma was knitting, as usual, her face dourly placid. But my mother was tight-lipped and flushed, and I guessed that she had been protesting vainly against Grandma's treatment of Uncle Ronald.

About five my father came home. As he dropped into

his chair I saw his eyes rest curiously on my mother's face. Then he turned to Grandma.

"Well?" he said. "How's your fiancé doing?"

"I couldn't say, Robert," replied Grandma austerely. "I haven't laid eye on him this day." She looked at my mother. "That reminds me, Jessie: There hasn't been a cheep out of him all afternoon. I have a notion you'd do well to go up and see how he is."

"Why?" My mother eyed her suspiciously. "What makes you say that?"

"Maybe I've got second-sight," said Grandma, and again I had the feeling that for some reason she was vastly amused by the whole situation.

"Yes, go ahead, Jess." My father was watching Grandma. "Something tells me you'd better."

My mother hesitated, frowning, and then got up and left the room. Less than a minute later I heard her running down the stairs, and she came bursting into the room, a sheet of paper in her hand.

"He's gone!" she cried. "He's gone! And will you listen to this: 'Dear Robert and Jessie, I'm off to Dumfries on the first train but am forced to leave most of my things behind. Will you be good enough to send them after me? And you can tell Mrs. Guthrie that she needn't follow me. Mrs. O'Toole is with me as I write and we're getting married as soon as we get to Dumfries. Your loving uncle, Ronald.' " She lowered the paper. "How on earth did he manage it? Mrs. O'Toole must have been here."

"He didn't manage anythin'!" said Grandma. "I went to town this mornin' and had a talk with Mrs. O'Toole, a pleasant wee body. While we were havin' lunch she came to the back door and Mary slipped her upstairs. Then your uncle did what I jaloused he'd do—chose the lesser of two evils."

My parents were staring at her, their faces slack with astonishment.

"So that was the whispering I heard?" my mother said. "But, Mamma, you told us distinctly that you intended to marry him yourself."

"I did not," said Grandma. "I said I was after marriage, but I didn't say whose."

"Well, you certainly meant us to think you were going to marry him," my mother said. "And I can't see why."

"Then I'll tell you, Jessie. I'd promised you he'd leave here without any ill-will toward either of you. But I know you, my bonnie: A good creature but none too bright. If you'd known the truth you'd never have been able to stick up for him the way you did, but as it is he's real pleased with you for takin' his part against me."

My father was looking at her with curiosity. "Not that I'm anything but grateful for the way you managed," he said. "But if Uncle Ronald was leaving here without us having to ask him, why were you so concerned with keeping his good will?"

Grandma snorted. "You're as bad's that wife of yours, Robert. Have you forgotten that you're his natural heir and that he's not goin' to live forever?"

GRANDMA
...and the Love-Blind

I HAD just passed my fourteenth birthday when I met Molly Mackay and, instantly, was smitten with what I was to recognize in later years as an acute case of puppy love. For some time previous to this rapturous, though by no means painless, experience I had been aware of a modification of my scornful attitude toward "lassies," a change that manifested itself in a new self-consciousness in their presence and in a new fastidiousness about my person. But until Molly came along the change had been general, unfocussed.

At the time of the meeting, the beginning of September, I had just got back from a summer in Ardrach with Grandma, and I knew nothing, therefore, of the Mackays' occupancy of the new house at the upper end of Kilburnie Road or of the scandalized whispering among the local ladies provoked by Molly, the Mackays' one and only child.

On this first morning of the new term I was plodding my way, slowly and reluctantly, toward school when behind me I heard the swift patter of footsteps. I turned. It was a girl, a stranger, carrying a schoolbag. She was older than I, a pretty girl with large soft innocent brown eyes and long brown curls. As she came up to me she smiled, demurely yet with the cool assurance of one who finds herself in a new but not unfamiliar situation.

"Hello!" she said. "You goin' to the Academy?"

The smile, through some strange chemistry, had done something to me, and as we walked on I felt my face burning. "Uh-huh," I mumbled.

"Good. So'm I. What's your name?"

"Du-duncan," I stammered.

"Du-duncan?" I could hear the grin in her voice. "Just Du-duncan?"

My confusion deepened. "Duncan Mackinley."

"Mackinley? Huh!" Her tone rejected all Mackinleys. "I'm a Mackay — Molly Mackay. The Mackays were a chieftain clan, you know." She giggled. "They tell me the Mackinleys were mostly tatie-hawkers."

A year before, I would have retorted that the Mackays were nothing but a lot of sheep-stealers who existed by preying on the Mackinley flocks, but already I was too deeply enamoured of this bewitching damsel to think of opposing her on behalf of my ancestors.

"I don't know anythin' about clans," I said humbly. I was silent then, screwing up my courage. "Will you be goin' home at noon?" I ventured finally.

"Of course. Why?"

"I—I thought maybe I could walk home with you."

"Oh, did you?" She was amused. "What for?"

"I just thought I—I'd like to."

"I know. But why?"

I was crimson now. "I wanted us to be—to be friends."

"Friends?" She giggled again. "You don't mean somethin' else, do you?"

I had, of course, meant something else, but nothing on earth could have made me put a name to it. I was still fumbling desperately for a way out when she spoke again, her voice full of laughter.

"What if some of the other boys want to be friends with me?"

My heart sank as I thought of my schoolmates, most of them so much more handsome and dashing than my own plump stocky self. A thoroughly detestable lot, they seemed to me

143

all of a sudden. "Maybe none of 'em will," I said, clutching at hope.

"Maybe not." Her tone implied that such a thing was highly improbable. "We'll see what we see."

I saw, all right. Almost every boy in the school, it seemed to me, wanted to be "friends with her," and even on the way home to lunch I had to share her with Findlay Hamilton, once my boon companion, but now a cad of the first water. Fortunately, Findlay lived near the Plantation, so I had her to myself the rest of the way up Kilburnie Road. And after lunch I waited for her and had her to myself again on the way back to school. But when school got out Findlay attached himself to us again like a human barnacle and, despite my scowls and mutterings, hung on until we were more than halfway home. And Molly, I noted with despair, did nothing at all to discourage him.

"Bloomin' rotter!" I muttered, as we continued up Kilburnie Road.

Molly turned wide innocent eyes on me. "Who, Dunc? Me?"

"No, Findlay," I said sulkily. "Why did you not get rid of him?"

"Get rid of him!" Her voice was high with surprise. "How could I, Dunc? I couldn't be rude."

"You could have let him see you didn't want him without bein' rude."

She raised her firm chin. "But that would have hurt his feelin's," she said righteously. "And it's not ladylike to be unkind to people." She sighed. "My, it's such a nuisance havin' boys I don't care for followin' me everyplace!"

And I believed her. Implicitly. And though I wasn't much of a fighting man, I decided that something would have to be done about Findlay Hamilton, that thorn in the tender flesh of fair womankind . . .

Held by my infatuation, I dallied so long at Molly's gate that my father was coming up the road from the station when I got back to the house. I waited for him and we went up the path together, his arm across my shoulders.

My mother was in the sitting room. As we walked in, her eyes went directly to me, and I saw with surprise that they

144

were dark with anger. Usually gentleness itself, it was almost shocking to see her so aroused.

"Well?" she demanded, ignoring my father. "Where have you been?"

"Just up the road," I said uneasily.

"Yes, up the road making sheep's eyes at that Mackay girl. I saw you going by. Looking like a sick calf!"

I blushed. "I was not. I was just crackin' with her."

My father, who had dropped into his chair, chuckled softly.

"Robert!" My mother turned stormy eyes on him. "It's not funny."

He sobered, obviously taken aback. "Well, maybe not, lass. But it's surely not that serious either, is it?"

"You don't know what you're talking about. It is so serious. It's very serious."

My father looked at her wonderingly. "But, Jess, the boy's going on fifteen. We've got to expect this kind of thing, have we not?"

"Not with her. Not with a girl two years older than him, a girl without any home discipline, a girl with a reputation like hers."

My father's eyebrows lifted. "I wouldn't think she'd been here long enough to get a reputation."

"Well, she has. And what's more, Mrs. Oliphant has a sister in Inverardie, where the Mackays come from, and she told Mrs. Oliphant that the girl was a notorious flirt, and worse than a flirt."

"She's not a flirt," I ventured to protest. "It's just that chaps won't leave her alone."

"Indeed?" my mother said acidly. "And of course you heard her ask them to leave her alone?"

"No, I didn't," I admitted. "Because she's too kind to. She says it's not ladylike to be unkind to people."

My father gave a little strangled snort, and I saw that his face was pink with suppressed laughter.

"Yes, laugh, Robert Mackinley!" my mother said furiously. "Make a joke of it! But I'm telling you this — if he doesn't leave this girl alone she'll end up by doing him a mischief. For she's not only a flirt but a malicious little trouble-maker with a nasty vicious streak in her."

145

"Oh?" My father stroked his cheek. "Do you know that for sure, Jess?"

"Yes, I know it for sure. Besides, I've met her and it's not hard to see what she is—far too sweet and smooth and innocent to be wholesome. Robert, I positively insist that Duncan keeps away from her."

My father nodded, though a little unwillingly, it seemed to me. "All right, Jess." He turned to me. "You heard your mother, Dunc. From now on you'll leave the Mackay girl severely alone."

A sense of disaster gripped me. "But I can't just leave her alone," I protested. "What if she wants to walk home with me?"

My father hesitated. "Well, I suppose you can't stop her. But mind you this—there's to be no dilly-dallying on the way. You'll be home ten minutes after you leave school, both at noon and in the afternoon. And in the evenings and on Saturday you'll stay in sight of the house. Is that clear?"

"Yes," I mumbled, and hung my head. It was only too clear. I was to be torn from my true love, the victim of blind prejudice and a ruthless parental tryanny . . .

It was ten minutes to nine the next morning before my mother would allow me to leave the house, too late for me to meet Molly. The Academy had separate playgrounds for boys and girls, so it was noon before I saw her. She was one of a mixed group milling around the main gate when I came out from the boys' entrance. At sight of me she came over, her eyes curious.

"What happened to you this mornin', Dunc? Were you late?"

Just then the ubiquitous Findlay joined us, and I shook my head. Her eyes darted at him and she gave a little nod of comprehension.

Findlay left us at the Plantation, and we started up Kilburnie Road, Molly almost trotting to keep up with my hurried stride.

"My conscience," she complained, "it's in an awful hurry you are. Slow up, Dunc."

"I can't," I said. "From now on I'm only allowed ten minutes to get to school and ten minutes to get home."

"Oh? So that was why I missed you this mornin'?"

146

"Yes."

"But why, Dunc?"

I was silent, wondering miserably what I was to tell her.

"I know!" Her voice came, sharp, shrewd. "It's somethin' to do with me?"

I nodded.

"They don't want you to be friends with me? Is that it?"

I nodded again.

"Why?" To my surprise there was a quiver of laughter in her voice. "Am I that scunnersome lookin'?"

I couldn't bring myself to tell her the truth. "My mother thinks you're too old for me."

She laughed suddenly, shrilly. "Yes, I eat wee boys!" Then curiously, "What if they see me walkin' with you now?"

"That doesn't matter," I said. "I can walk home with you. But that's all."

"Oh, you can?" As we slowed by my gate she laughed again, but softly, almost gloatingly. "Well, I suppose I'll have to make the most of it."

I was about to ask her what she meant when I saw that my mother was watching us from the sitting-room window. I glanced at Molly. She was staring back at my mother, her eyes narrowed in defiance. Then with a disdainful toss of her head she turned and walked away.

But after lunch, while I was in the sitting room with my mother, waiting for permission to go back to school, I discovered what Molly had meant.

"Duncan," my mother said suddenly, and pointed to the window, "what's the meaning of this?"

I looked past her and felt a tingle of pleasure as I saw Molly standing by the gate.

"She's waitin' on me," I said with unconcealed gratification.

"I can see that. But how does she know you haven't left for school?"

A little huffily, I told her what had passed between us on the way home.

"I see." She looked back at the window, her gentle mouth compressed. "So now she's out to make trouble, the malicious little gypsy."

"She is not," I defended Molly. "She's doin' it because she likes me."

147

"Likes you!" My mother swung around, her eyes flashing. "Oh, you—you simpleton!"

I said nothing. There was no use trying to reason with prejudice. . . .

For the next week or so my love affair followed the same pattern. Every noon and afternoon I would walk home with Molly, and in the mornings and after lunch I would find her waiting faithfully at the gate for me. And though she asked me frequently how my mother was taking it and giggled glee-fully when I told her, I refused to believe that she was acting out of anything but fondness of myself.

But my bliss was far from being complete. The evenings, usually only too short, seemed endless now, and I would gloom around the house, heavy of heart and yearning for the company of my heart's desire.

Then late one afternoon Grandma arrived on the scene.

"My soul!" she remarked as we sat down to tea. "What's up with this callant of yours, Jessie? A body would think he was ready to burst out greetin'."

"He's madly in love," my mother said with cold satire.

"Is he, now?" Grandma examined me with dour interest. "Aye, he has that thrawn peely-wally look. Who's the fair charmer?"

"A sweet young thing called Molly Mackay," my mother said, and went on to give Grandma what I considered to be an entirely inaccurate and uncharitable description of Molly's person and character.

"Aye, I know the kind of fliskmahoy. They're no rarity, I'm sorry to say. But, ach, he's got to learn, I suppose."

"Not from her," my mother said sharply, and described the measures she had taken to control the situation.

By the time she had finished Grandma was sitting back in her chair, her lean bony face forbidding.

"My faith, girl," she barked, "have you gone daft altogether?"

"What?" My mother lifted startled eyes. "Daft?"

"Aye, just that. My, I wonder at you, Jessie. Thirty-seven years of age, and still you know nothin' about bairns."

"But I — I don't understand," stammered my mother. "You're surely not proposing that I allow him to associate with this — this creature any more than I have to?"

148

"Indeed, I am," said Grandma. "Within limits, of course. As you well know, Jessie, I've never been one to let a bairn run wild, but there's a world of difference between keepin' an eye on him and wrappin' him in cotton wool. You'll do your laddie just as much harm with too much attention as you will with too little."

"I don't care." My mother's mouth was set obstinately. "I won't have it. I'm his mother and it's my duty to protect himself from himself."

"Jessie," said Grandma gently, "do you mind, when you were fourteen, a rascally wee callant—Rab—used to deliver the groceries—Rab Quinn?"

"Mamma!" My mother had turned scarlet. "For any sake!"

"Aye, I see you do," said Grandma meaningly.

My father grinned. "Ah-hah!" he said. "What happened with Rab Quinn?"

"Nothin' that concerns you, Robert," said Grandma rebukingly. "But, Jessie, you'll understand why I mention him?"

My mother was chewing her lower lip. "That was different. Quite different."

"Don't blether, girl!" snapped Grandma. "It was no different. The whole thing is, you're lettin' your feelin's run away with you — swimmin' like mad against the tide when common sense should tell you you ought to be swimmin' with it."

"I agree with your mother, Jess," my father said. "I've thought from the beginning you were making too much of this business."

My mother threw him a look of mingled anger and reproach. "Very well," she said in the voice of one betrayed. "Have it your own way. Let this little hussy do as she likes with him. But just as sure as death she'll do him an injury, and then I hope the pair of you will be satisfied."

"I'm sure we will, Jessie," said Grandma. "And you too."

Which, judging from my mother's face, made as little sense to her as it did to me. . . .

As was to be expected, I lost no time the next morning in telling Molly the good news, but was disappointed in her reaction to it.

"What made them change their minds?" she said, and

against all reason I had the feeling that she was displeased somehow.

"Grandma did," I said. "She thought they weren't treatin' me fair."

She made no reply but as we walked on I was aware of a new coolness in her manner, a coolness that became more marked as the day went on. And that afternoon when we started for home I found to my chagrin that Findlay, who had dropped out of the running, was back in favour and was to accompany us.

"Cheeky brute!" I muttered in exasperation when, at last, he left us. "I ought to bash him one."

She slipped her arm through mine and, for the first time since morning, smiled at me. "Why don't you, Dunc?" she said, her eyes sparkling. "It'd be the price of him."

But it wasn't Findlay, really, I was annoyed at. "There'd be no need," I said sullenly, "if you wouldn't be so nice to him."

"Duncan Mackinley!" she protested. "That's not fair. Just because I'm civil is no reason for him to take advantage, is it?"

I made no reply. My beloved, I knew, wasn't being honest, but it was better to say nothing than risk a breach by arguing about it.

The next day was Saturday. As usual I was kept one way and another for the first part of the morning, but as soon as I was free I went along the road to Molly's house and whistled. After a moment the door opened and she came out on the stoop.

"Hello." She didn't smile. "What is it?"

"I thought maybe you'd like to take a daunder."

"Oh? Where to?"

"Brodie's farm. Follow the burn and come back by road."

Her nose wrinkled. "Ach, what's the good of that?"

"We could see the cows and things," I said lamely. "And Dave's pony."

"Dave?" Interest dawned in her eyes. "Who's he?"

"Dave Brodie. The son. He used to go to the Academy but he works with his father now."

Her face had brightened. "All right, Dunc. I like ponies. Just a jiffy till I get my coat."

"Duncan, take a look at yourself in the mirror."

We didn't follow the burn to Brodie's farm. Molly was so eager to see the pony that we went by road and in half an hour walked into the U-shaped barnyard. By the milkroom door a barefooted milkmaid was washing down the steps, and I asked her where Dave was.

"I'm no sure," she said. "He went ower tae Fernie wi' the dogcairt this mornin' an' I doot he's no' back yet. But ye could tak' a look around."

I looked at Molly and saw that the animation had left her face.

"We can see the pony, just the same, Molly," I said consolingly. "It's in a box-stall in the stable."

She gave a little indifferent shrug but followed me across the yard and into the stable. To my surprise Dave was there, sitting on a feed bin, reassembling a set of horse clippers he had been oiling.

"Hey, Dunc," he said. "How's the boy?" His eyes moved to Molly. "Who's this? Your best girl?"

I flushed. "She's Molly Mackay, Dave. She lives near me."

Dave grinned at her appreciatively, his teeth very white against his bronzed face. "Jinkins!" he said. "Some people have all the luck." He worked the clippers. "Molly, how would you like a clippin'? I see your hair's a wee thing on the long side."

Molly laughed gaily, her good spirits restored. "No, thanks. I like it this way. Better try Dunc, here. He needs a haircut."

I felt at the back of my head. True enough, I did need a haircut. But not, I thought, with any horse clippers. "I'll do till I get to the barber," I said.

"Oh, go on, Dunc." Molly's eyes were sparkling. "Let Dave do it."

"Aye, come on, Dunc," said Dave. "I'll do you a first-class job."

I shook my head. "Not me, thanks."

"Ach, don't be so obstinate," Molly said impatiently. She pointed to a team of Clydesdales in a nearby stall. "Look at these horses' manes — just as even as even. I bet Dave can do better than any old barber. Or are you feared?"

152

"Feared!" scoffed Dave. "Not him. He doesn't know the meanin' of the word. Come on, Dunc, and I'll trim you up."

Reluctantly, yet anxious to deserve his praise, I went over and let him apply the clippers to my head. And as he worked Molly stood watching, her eyes very bright with what I took to be interest. At last it was over and Dave stood back and admired his handiwork.

"My, but there's a braw job," he said. "I'm real proud of myself. What do you think, Molly?"

"Oh, it's perfect." There was a little tremor in Molly's voice. Of admiration, I thought. "That must be the best haircut he's ever had."

I rubbed experimentally at the back of my head. The hair felt even and crisp, as after a visit to the barber. "You're sure it's all right?" I said to Molly.

"I should say it is!" There was an odd stiffness about her lips. "I never saw anythin' like it."

"Aye, I'm an artist, that's what I am." Chuckling, Dave put the clippers on a shelf and then took out his watch. "Twenty-five to one. . . . Molly, how'd you like a ride on my pony?"

"Twenty-five to one!" I exclaimed. "I've got to go home. Come on, Molly."

Molly turned. "But, Dunc—" She stopped abruptly and, to my astonishment, began to shriek with laughter. I watched her blankly as she rocked to and fro, her face contorted, then turned to Dave.

"What's she laughin' at?"

He didn't answer me. He was looking at Molly, mirth filling his face. Suddenly he let out a guffaw and they both stood there, whooping.

I watched them, puzzled and vexed. "What's so funny?" I demanded.

Molly was recovering now. "Y-you," she gasped. "Wantin' to go home before . . . before we've even seen the p-pony!"

I smiled feebly. What was so terribly funny about that? "Well, come on," I said. "Let's go."

"I'm stayin', Dunc." She was dabbing at her eyes. "I don't need to be home at any special time."

153

"But—" I stopped short. There was no valid objection to her staying that I could make.

"Don't fash yourself, Dunc," Dave grinned. "I'll see she gets home in good shape."

Suspicion hit me then. Was it for the pony's sake she was staying or for Dave's? I couldn't be sure, but in either case there was nothing I could do about it.

"Well, I'm away," I said sourly and, without saying good-bye, walked from the stable.

I was halfway across the yard when behind me I again heard Molly's screeching laughter. "Daft," I muttered. "Lassies are all daft." . . .

Kilburnie Road was quiet at that time on a Saturday and the only person I met on my way home was Constable Angus Macphail. I wondered, as I passed him, why he should stop short and gape at me, but he said nothing so I kept on going. By the time I got to the house I had forgotten the slight incident.

I found Grandma and my parents in the sitting room.

"So there you are," my mother said. "You're just in time—" Something like horror came into her face. "Oh, my gracious!" she said faintly.

"Great Scott!" My father was staring at me as if I were something leprous. "What in the blazes have you done to yourself?"

"What?" I looked wonderingly from them to Grandma. She was watching me, her deep-set eyes gleaming.

"Tell me, laddie," she said. "Who cut your hair?"

"Dave Brodie," I said. "Why, Grandma?"

"Did you ask him to do it?"

"No. Molly did. She said I needed a haircut and he did it with the horse clippers."

"I knew it!" my mother said, and looked accusingly at Grandma. "I told you something like this would happen!"

"So did I know it," said Grandma with dour calm. "But I didn't dare hope it would be this soon."

"Hope!" my mother said with incredulity. "Good gracious, Mamma, you surely don't mean to say—"

"Ach, wheesht, lassie!" said Grandma testily. "You weary me with your dreich yammerin'." She turned to me. "Duncan, take a look at yourself in the mirror."

154

I went over to the mirror. Consternation gripped me. Except for a narrow plume of hair along the middle of my head, I was practically bald! And now I remembered, and understood, the Constable's slack-jawed stare. Then the memory of Molly's unaccountable laughter returned to me and rage and chagrin burned through me.

"Duncan," Grandma said. I turned away from the grotesque object in the mirror and saw that the gleam was still in her eyes. "You'll not deny it," she said. "She's a great one for a baur, this lass of yours?"

"She's no lass of mine!" I raged, between anger and tears. "I'm done with her! Her and her big brown eyes! She's nothin' but a rotten two-faced sneaky—"

"That'll do!" Grandma raised her hand. "You're not tellin' us anythin' we didn't know." She looked at my mother. "Well, Jessie?" she said blandly.

"Oh, I know." I could hear relief in my mother's voice. "You were right, of course. But his hair, Mamma!" she lamented. "His bonnie hair—"

"Ach, his hair!" said Grandma. "His hair'll grow. But I warrant you he'll not forget in a hurry the lesson he's just learned."

And, as usual, she was quite right.

155

Date Due

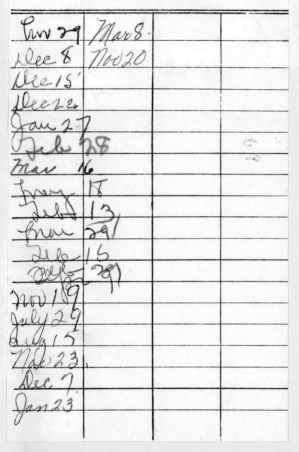

Nov 29	Mar 8.		
Dec 8	Nov 20		
Dec 15			
Dec 22			
Jan 27			
Feb 28			
Mar 16			
May 18			
Feb 13			
Mar 29			
Dec 15			
Sep 29			
Nov 19			
July 29			
Aug 15			
Nov 23			
Dec 7			
Jan 23			